The Blue Pearl

by Kevin Boileau

also by **Kevin Boileau**

Theory

Genuine Reciprocity and Group Authenticity
First Edition

The Algebra of History (*with David A. Boileau*)

Essays on Phenomenology and the Self

Coming 2013
Radical Subjectivity

Literary

A Reason and A Season

The Patient

EPIS Press
31 Fort Missoula Road #4
Missoula, MT 59804
epispublishing1@gmail.com

Heart-of-Fire is an imprint of
EPIS Press

The Heart-of-Fire name and logo are
trademarks of EPIS Press

Printed in the United States of America
First Edition October 2012

Cover Design: Tia Hopkins
Inside Cover: Joanna Gorham

ISBN 978-0-9849512-2-2

The Blue Pearl

Preface

We had all tried to reach it, somewhere in the darkness just around
the corner. It had been this way forever. That feeling of longing. The
object of desire that is always there beyond our grasp. The feeling
of never being satisfied. We had never gotten to that gentle place of
repose toward which we all gravitate. I, personally, had never been
there either.

So I drifted forward, being driven in various ways toward the
objects of my affection…the stand-ins that we create as substitutions
for the imperfect early days, and the substructures upon which our
projects rest. On occasion we all drift off course, and I had too,
especially after I'd lost contact with him.

The last time there'd been an awkward distance between us.
There had been no closure and I had just drifted on. I was tired of
considering and jaded in my reflections. On top of that, there was
the rupture.

PART

ONE

Chapter 1

There was a regular pumping-swooshing sound coming into the left side. There were white coats and a bright light above. The air was still. My feet were tucked under a series of sheets and blankets. There were voices and an unfamiliar smell.

There was a pounding sensation that throbbed in concert with the pumping-swooshing sound. First the throb. Then the pumping. Up and down, back and forth with regularity. Along with the light it hurt.

The white coats were moving fast. Barking orders. Responding. Carrying instruments and handing them to others. The voices were talking about the problem. It was serious. They were talking about the serious problem and scuttling about because of it.

The throbbing, the light, and the movements had blended together and were now disentangling themselves from each other, separating into their own discrete elements. The overhead light became clearer, its edges and textures refining into several layers and dimensions of plastic and metal.

One of the voices became more distinct. It came closer and louder. Then, there were words. I tried to sit up. I tried to wrestle myself free of the sheets and the needles and the pumping-swooshing in my ear. Sir, she said. You must lay back. Try not to move. Everything will be okay. You're doing fine.

What? I asked. Where am I?

She took my hand and spoke. Mr. Lykeman, please try to remain calm.

You've had a major rupture.

What do you mean, a major rupture?

I can't tell you much right now but the doctor will be in later to speak with you.

I tried to move but she gently held me back.

You mustn't move, she said. Try to remain still. You're in the hospital.

We did this for what seemed an eternity, a folie a deux of she suggesting and me resisting, or oppositely, me entreating and she countering. I tried to raise my head up off the pillow to see what was around me but she continued her encouragements that I should lay back and rest.

Finally, in utter exhaustion, I relented and fell asleep to murmured voices and a medley of bright light, white colors, and swooshing sounds that eventually all gelled together into a nondescript nothingness.

Then it was dark and quiet and the voices were gone.

The next day I awoke to a doctor leaning over me, reading my chart, uttering uh, huh… okay… uh huh, until I stirred. Then I felt his hand on my wrist and heard him speak.

Mr. Lykeman, he said. I struggled to open my eyes.

Mr. Lykeman, he repeated. Do you know where you are?

My lips felt dry and chapped and I smacked them together.

Water, I said, opening my eyes, looking for a sink.

He quickly brought a half-filled cup of water to my lips, which I quickly dashed all over my face. He brought me another.

I opened my eyes and looked into his. I must be in a hospital, I said.

He nodded his head up and down, assenting.

You've had a major rupture, he said.

Christ, I've heard that before, I thought. What in the hell? I asked.

A rupture, he said. It was a total destruction of your previous system and orientation. Everything is out of whack, he added.

I looked around the room. Still there was the swooshing-pumping sound. My heart? I asked. Lungs?

Nothing like that, he replied. Then he left me to my exhaustion and the quiet, except for the sounds of medical personnel scurrying about out in the hallway.

I again fell asleep to a concatenation of images from my childhood, my current life at the Company, and a salty-numb taste of watered-down soup and saltines they'd given me for a late breakfast.

A television hung on the wall in front of me with news about the Middle East. No respite here. The volume was turned all the way down, but I could see the images of the soldiers and the dead. I looked away again, spotting the machine pump that had been disconnected from me but which was still in the room. A sort of IV was in my arm but it seemed different from the ones I'd had in the past.

Then I heard the scratching at the window. At first, I wasn't sure if it was in my head or not, but it continued. Not continuously, more intermittently. Scratch, scratch, then a light ping. Then I saw it so it must've been Real.

It was a large raven with blue iridescent feathers looking right at me. I could see the acute, beady eyes looking right at me as it stood right in the windowsill.

His eyes, my eyes, total connection. No sound. I felt like I was being pulled right out of the bed, without resistance. He just stood there looking, holding something in his mouth.

The rich blue iridescence was mesmerizing, dark eyes capturing my gaze, unmoving mass. I didn't move and I could hardly breathe. I'd heard the stories about birds who'd come to take humans to the dead, and I didn't want to go there. I wanted to go back to my life at the office.

You've had a major rupture, Mr. Lykeman. It was pounding out a massive headache again for me and I didn't want to be taken by the raven. So I pulled the sheet higher over my chin and remained motionless.

The raven hopped around the sill a bit, still penetrating right into me with its gaze and then without warning left. I looked over at the windowsill and he was gone. Then for some inexplicable reason, I dragged myself and the IV over to the window and saw it. There was something it had left on the sill. It was bluish in color.

With what strength and motor skill I had left, I was able to jar the window frame upward enough to grab the blue object. I grabbed it with my hand and dragged myself back into bed. Only when I was safely under the covers did I open my hand:

It was a rounded, oval-shaped, blue pearl. I'd seen these before a few times in my life, I think, and I was sure that it was a real one. The raven had left me a blue pearl. I squeezed it with my hand and fell asleep, just as the medical staff re-entered my room to talk to me about my rupture.

Since they thought I was asleep they talked amongst themselves quietly but I heard them anyway. I've never seen such a rupture like this, one said. It was total and utter, another said. Recovery on these can take a long time — forever, the loudest of the male voices said.

I slept, carrying on my fragmented dream, the small blue ball safe in my clenched palm.

A couple of days later, the doctors released me from the hospital based on my promise not to exacerbate my condition. They had it covered over pretty good with bandages and tape and implored me not to remove it. I assented and left with the antiseptic for a few days at home; then it would be back to the office.

I was supposed to rest at home, but I was so used to going to the office 6 days a week that after one day at home I got up early in the morning and went to the office. I shaved. I showered. I picked out the best-pressed suit I had and went to the office. I was a company man. I was an Organization Man.

It'd been like this from the first day I'd been a bright-eyed, bushy-tailed youngster with a college degree. I'd intended on working in the financial services sector with the hope that some of it would come back to my own bank account. As it was, they had me just where they wanted me and I knew it. And they gave me just enough to keep me from walking away out of fear.

My work had become regular and I was good at it. The number crunching and the bean counting I'd been trained for, and by now I knew all the techniques and the protocols. There wasn't anything that I didn't know about my job.

Well, that first day back I got a few surprised looks from the staff, but mostly it was the warm and friendly welcome back into the numbing safety of the time clock and the workday.

The company was old but we'd moved into a new building in the last few years and modernized all of our equipment so everything still had a fresh smell that invited production. The lights in the breakroom were obnoxious, however, being so bright and penetrating that it was all we could do to get our lunches in and out of the microwave and back to our workstations.

Parking was easy. I'd go right into the space and up the elevator into my department. Someone had obviously spent a great deal of time and energy creating a workflow structure that encouraged work and discouraged loitering.

That first day back I popped a couple of the pills that my regular psychiatrist had prescribed for me, or maybe from the nurse practitioner whom I saw on the side when the psychiatrist wouldn't give me anymore. Anyway, that first day back I drank two cups of coffee and popped the pills right off, which put me back into the right mind space so I could do my job. I did this for the next several days, drinking the coffee and taking the pills — eating my regular lunch, meeting my time deadlines and eating the pills.

I was uneasy. Even with the pharmaceuticals it was becoming more difficult to get to the office. It's not that I was disheartened or depressed [well not more than the usual], but my body felt different. It felt askew, my heart's rhythm, the way I stepped into the world, walked to my car and up to my work station and all. And it was growing, the gnawing of it all. The grating and gnawing of it all was getting to me.

One day not too long after I came back from the hospital I saw her walking down the hallway, her dark business suit pressed to the maximum and that string of pearls around her neck. I don't know what came over me, but when she walked by I jumped on top of her like a wild monkey, at once trying to rip the Tahitian blues from her and bite and cut her with my nails and my teeth.

I was like a rabid dog-monkey totally out of control but not really dangerous. As such, it only took two coworkers to strip me off the VP, and escort me down to the lunchroom where someone injected me with a hypodermic needle. I was then able to start relaxing as they told me to eat my sandwich and that the company doctor was coming to take care of me.

I ate my sandwich and the doctor ["doc" we called him a bit paternalistically, because he was mostly just a pill pusher] came and treated me. I was all day in his office, got a new prescription, apologized to the VP [she understood!} and then I was sent home. All was back to order at the company.

Two weeks came and went and I still did not unwrap my rupture, in line the with doctor's orders. It felt hot on the inside of the wrapping, mysterious and heated. Even in the midst of my expected and predictable schedule, though, I was curious about why I was not supposed to uncover the rupture.

Evidently the company doctor had been in touch with the ER team and so we had appointments scheduled over the next few months for my "wellbeing." I was not supposed to uncover the rupture at this time, but every morning I got up and every late afternoon when I got home, I religiously went to the mantel and looked at the small, blue mystery that the raven had set carefully upon my windowsill at the hospital. In my imaginations about it, I couldn't detect a clearly definable path. In contrast, there was a pathless whole without boundary or time.

I'd pick it up and hold it in my hand until I felt the heat. Then I'd put it back down abruptly, and go back to my routine: the laundry, the dishes, the sweeping and the mopping; the letters, the groceries, and the dry cleaning. These were all the things that got me from 6 a.m. until 6 p.m. in such a way that my life was expectable and easy.

On occasion I'd get all my chores done and there'd still be time left in the day. At those times, I'd be fit to be tied, so I'd pop another "calming" pill. I had another encounter, again, just a few weeks after I was in the emergency room.

I'd just finished dinner and all the work was done. I was sitting in the big easy chair right in front of the television watching the news: more killings, people starving, and wars. I'd read all of the books on my shelves so there wasn't anything there for me. So I just sat until I felt pulled to the mantel.

I sat in my chair and looked at the stone ledge where the blue pearl was. I looked up at the pearl on the mantel like I did every night and several times a day. I didn't get up. Instead, I sat there and felt the pull. I couldn't quite see it but I knew it was there. There was a fire burning. Candles were burning. And I sat in my chair, replaying the events of the past several weeks. It was me and the endless reflection of the pathless, empty confrontation with my past.

I'd been in a park sitting on a bench when she'd walked by. It wasn't romantic and I wasn't attracted to her, but there was a deep, compelling pull. She'd looked at me with sadness and in that moment the park turned from green to dark gray, like a cemetery, and all was frozen in time. Then, my daytime dream was interrupted by a noise.

Tap, tap, tap. There was something at my kitchen window so I was temporarily distracted from the daydream. I got up with a start as the tapping continued. I got to the kitchen. I looked out the window. Nothing there. I froze motionless and waited for it. Nothing. So I went back to the memory at the park and fell asleep.

I woke up the next day still sitting on my chair in front of the pearl, still thinking about the woman I had seen in the park. She always walked alone in the afternoons. She walked alone in the park and I would especially notice her because no one else was around. It was quiet like a cemetery. I'd sit there on a bench and watch her, slightly hunched over, making her way step-by-step, quietly.

Wearing dark blue or black, or gray she'd make her way around the park while I watched. She'd walk the worn-down dirt path, around and around the park, perhaps 2 or 3 times, never once looking up. I'd wait until she left and then I'd sit there on the bench for a while longer until the clouds came. Then I'd leave just before the rain.

This is how my life went. Sitting in front of the mantel watching the pearl, hoping I'd hear the tapping noise at the window [I wondered if it were the same raven that had come to the hospital]. Jogging my old car down to the park just after the lunch crowd had left and she'd shown up. Getting letters and phone calls from the office, including the company doctor.

They wanted me back. At first the notes were encouraging and friendly, expressing condolences at my rupture, but as I returned fewer and fewer of them, the tones started to change. Even my secretary's attitude started to change from loyalty to consternation to exasperation. Then I got a letter from the Vice-President upon whom I had jumped.

Dear Mr. Lykeman, she had started. "I am hoping that you get the help that you so desperately need. I know that everyone in your department misses you greatly. The company doctor thinks he can help you but you don't return his calls. Please consider doing so. It would be to your benefit. Warmly, ______.

So the letters stacked up and the voicemails continued, but still I did nothing except sit on the chair and wait for the tapping.

Then one day I woke up to the sun. I got out of bed. I went to the chair and drank old coffee that I heated up on the stove. I sat and stared at the pearl. I sat in front of the pearl and stared.

The sunlight came in through the half-opened blinds right up to my face. Right to my eyes, blocking most of my vision of the mantel and the pearl that sat there. My vision became fragmented with slices of refracted sun penetrating my optic nerve as a series of shattered perspectives on my life. And just at that time, I could start to hear the tapping again, unsure whether it was coming from the kitchen window or somewhere in my head.

Tap, tap, tap. I turned and saw nothing. I turned back to the fragmented rays of morning sun coming through the window as I sat in the darkened room. I wasn't sure whether I was hearing things again or whether it was real. I wasn't sure whether it was that raven from the hospital but I got up when I heard the sound again. I got up and went to the kitchen and he was there.

It was the raven with the blue iridescence sitting there on the windowsill. He was just standing there looking at me with both the iridescence and the sun, while I hovered there weightless. It was the raven who'd been at the hospital.

My palms started to sweat and my head became heavy.

I couldn't see much except for the sun and the iridescence.

The phone rang but I didn't answer it. Still, the raven stood there without moving.

I poured myself a coffee at the kitchen table and sat down. The
raven did not move. The coffee was hot and burned my lips but
I continued drinking it while watching the raven who continued
standing still.

We looked at each other as I sipped the hot, dark-brown fluid. I still
had the bandages around my wound and I was too scared to take
them off. I didn't want to see the effects of this so-called rupture.
I just wanted it to heal and for the doctor to take the bandages off
when he thought it was time. After that I'd go back to work.

After I finished the coffee while sitting alone in the yellow-toned
kitchen, the sun streaming in and thereby accentuating that
aloneness, I stood up. I did so to alleviate the uncanniness. I went
to the living room and retrieved the Tahitian blue pearl from the
mantel. I brought it into the kitchen, trying to see the intricacies that
were hidden from the capacity of my eyes, without success.

The raven stood still and watched as I sat down again at the table,
placing the pearl in front of me on the table. I sat and he watched.
I leaned back in the chair, pushing my feet out in front of me. Even
though there was caffeine running around in my brain, I started to
drift off. The cool, midmorning air was coming in the window along
with the sun, and I felt outside of myself though safe with the raven
staring at me.

I fell asleep.

Chapter 2

There was a foul, sick smell of vomit and shit when we got to the
house. When we opened the door we could see dried blood on the
floor. She was lying there in a pool of her own red liquid, stiff from
rigor, blocking the door. We didn't want to touch her so we went
around back. We came up through the basement and could see that
the pets were emaciated and dead. There were maggots crawling all
over one of the pups and a cat stretched out in front of a dried-up
water dish.

We called the authorities right away. They didn't take long to send
the fire trucks, the police, and the medical examiner, confirming
right away that she had been murdered. According to the official
report, she had been strangled, stabbed multiple times, and hit over
the head with a large, blunt object. She had been dead for several
days. Somebody had left an unreadable message on the living room
wall with a black pen.

It was summer on the Island, which brought a number of temporary
residents who lived elsewhere for the colder months but who
congregated here every year. During a complete cycle of seasons,
the mood oscillated between the excitement of summer vacation and
the quiet, peaceful splashing of the waves after all the temporaries
had gone back home to the city.

The white seagulls were ubiquitous. You'd know them by their
raucous, hungry cries while diving in the air or eating garbage in
one of the alleys behind a long street lined with restaurants and bars.

Her name was Rachel. She'd come from a family that used to have
a lot of money but who lost most of it due to financial ineptitude,
graft, and bad luck. As far as she knew, all she had was a name and
a whole lot of history. The family grave was upstate in Ravenswood.

She was tall with a shapely body. Not taller than most men but taller
than the average woman. She had full lips and a clean complexion;

bright eyes with almost a regal posture. In her early teen days she'd hang out at the mall or at one of the local restaurants where you could get a cheap ice cream. In her early twenties, there was a subtle hardening of the fibers in her face. While her right eye remained direct and clear, there was a guardedness in her left eye, as if she were always holding something back.

She'd become something of a socialite. There were private primary schools, prep schools, and expensive colleges. She had two trust funds and a purse full of cash with which she paid for everything. When she was seventeen she bought a brand new BMW with some of it.

She always got men to do things against their will even when she was young. For example, she seduced one of her young college professors and then threatened to tell his wife and the school unless he gave her money and continued to see her. Or there was the time even earlier when she convinced the assistant headmaster at boarding school to give her a ride into town one Saturday morning. There were rumors that he had tried to force himself upon her and eventually he left for another school. It was because he wouldn't change her grade.

Her father was overly affectionate with her but nobody thought that anything untoward had ever happened. She was his favorite, one of five healthy children, and they had a private bond that no one could ever penetrate. Even at holiday homecomings she was still the life of the party, manipulating her brothers and their girlfriends until she got what she wanted. Even in a large room with a lot of people she and her father could always catch each other's eyes.

After she graduated college she took a job at one of the large marketing firms in the City. Large salary. Beautiful clothes. Popular. Dated a lot of men. Every chance she got she hopped a flight to the UK or to Europe. With a second degree in sociology (and an emphasis on human sexuality) she pursued several outlets: sex shops, lectures at the universities, books on perversity; she was even asked to do a radio show on dating.

She moved with celerity. Whether it was walking or shopping or putting together a project at work, she did it impeccably and she always did it efficiently. It was as if she had another appointment just around the corner. Like destiny was pulling at her.

She would look at herself in the mirror, noticing the lines on her face and the visible crow's feet at the outside edges of her eyes. She'd cup her breasts in her hands and turn away so she could see her backside. It was still tight and firm, the way the prep school boys had liked it. The way the college jocks had liked it. The way all the men she seduced and controlled had liked it. Even he still liked it.

She was forty-three years old and looked twenty-nine except for the hardness in her face and the holdback in that one eye. She was still lucky to be a part of the social set in which she grew up. After her family lost most of its fortune she cleaned out her accounts and flew off to Paris for several months. By the time she had returned, her grandparents had both passed away and her parents had filed for divorce.

After her family's financial downfall there were dark bags under her eyes. She smelled of alcohol and sweat. Her trademark laugh which always made everyone feel good because of its lightness and warmth had turned caustic and cynical. Even the corners of her mouth no longer turned upward, instead often pointing in tandem toward the ground, toward her shame.

A long time ago she'd read some of the letters that her grandfather, James Lyken, had written to the family. He had been living on the west coast, born and raised in New England but he'd moved. There'd been rumors about him. Real bad stories about him being a serial killer and all but no one every caught him and he never stood trial. Eventually, in his sixties, he had left the U.S. for Europe, and after the letters no one ever heard from him again. There had been a book about it, as well.

There was more intrigue to Rachel's story. As it turns out, one day a little girl was born, stillborn. When she came out she was dead so the parents hushed it all up and buried the little piece of human flesh, whose soul had other plans. Her mother died shortly thereafter of grief and complications. After the family got over the tragedy and little Rachel was quietly buried somewhere in the back part of the estate, her father got his private girlfriend pregnant and this time it took. Out of a kind of weird respect to the stillborn one they named the new baby Rachel and kept the secret safe while she grew up. Even though her father married the girlfriend this was more to legitimate her own feelings, but the marriage never integrated with his social circle.

They put her in a beautiful little room that always carried in the natural light. It was a golden natural light. It was across the hall and down from a door that was always locked. This locked door led into a room that was filled with old treasures—-paintings, artifacts and the like, from travels to far away destinations. But it also housed a few desks and old file cabinets, and was a great source of curiosity for her and two younger siblings as they grew up.

One day the kids jimmied the lock and looked around the darkened room. After her brother and sister got scared and left, Rachel continued looking around until she found the letters in the desk. She was a good reader and so with her flashlight found the documents from the hospital recording the stillborn. It was confusing for her at age nine to see documents with her name on them, describing that she was deceased. She never told anyone about them but she carried the revelation like a scarlet letter on her forehead. She was supposed to be dead.

After she got older we met in secret in one of the rooms of their mansion, or we'd go deep into the grounds of the estate until we were certain we were alone. Then we'd explore each other like a jigsaw puzzle, trying this piece and that until we were satisfied that we'd uncovered the code of romantic love. By thirteen we both experienced our first orgasm with each other. It was a magical world that we created.

In high school we lost touch except for holidays because we each went to different prep schools [me on scholarship, all the way from the west]. Hers was in Connecticut; mine in Massachusetts.

Christmas was always passionate, though, with the booze and the drugs, and her hot, young flesh next to mine. College was more of the same although we both had significant others so we had to sneak around.

As time wore on, we became more distant and saw each other less. I learned about her family's financial troubles as well as her addiction to speed and cocaine. Then I heard that she went away to Europe. She took all her money out of the bank, whatever was left from the trust funds after the series of bankruptcies and left.

At this time, she and I were not very close. I had moved on with my life and was planning to move to the west coast with my girlfriend. So I didn't keep tabs on her much. Then she seemed to vanish. The last I heard from her was when she wrote me from Paris, drunk. She was upset and lost, panicked over her family's change of fortune, something she'd shared with me only. Then all was silent.

Her family split up. Her parents divorced and her mother went back to the other side of town. People talked about them for several months until it was no longer interesting. Then she was silent and I never heard from her again, directly. Many years later, though, I heard through the grapevine that she had returned from overseas, resettled in New York. This was probably around twenty-five years later and she would be in her early forties.

Chapter 3

It was fall here on the Island. It was September and the mornings were getting colder. The murder had been top news for the past few weeks, but I think everyone was getting tired of this being the only thing to talk about.

The usual? she asked, waving a pot of coffee in the air with one hand, the other placing a steaming hot plate of food in front of the stranger who had sat down at the counter a few minutes ago.

That'd be fine, I said, opening the morning paper, hoping that the story was no longer front-page news. It wasn't. Instead there was more national news on the war and a column on the latest sex scandal in Washington.

She poured me a cup of black coffee. I looked around at the usual crowd at the diner, nodded hello a few times, and set about to read the paper and eat my breakfast. She set a plate of eggs and ham and toast in front of me and I dug right into it. I normally ate a large amount on Monday mornings before I headed down to my beach house at the shore where I'd set up a studio. When my work as a part-time accountant was boring [I had left my full-time career years earlier], I spent my time down at the studio painting and writing. Summer tourists bought my paintings so it was a good way to supplement my income.

I dug into the eggs and the ham and polished it all off with the toast and the coffee. I wiped my mouth with my flannel shirt, pulled out some bills, and headed out. See you, the waitress said.

It was cloudy and dark, and the streets were wet. Most of the tourists had left over the past few weeks so it was quiet around here again. It was melancholy, really, with the turn of seasons and the exodus. For the next several months it'd be quiet, except for the gulls, and the planes that'd fly overhead on local routes.

I was wearing my rubber boots today because it had rained a lot
lately, and they made a crunching sound as I headed down to the
docks. There was a machinist humming away in his garage. There
was a grocery delivery truck that'd made it on the first ferry. There
was also an affluent couple with an infant who were staying at the
Deluxe Hotel. I could see them walking up the street toward the
restaurants. They'd probably eat at "The Well-To-Do," which served
the same food as the diner, except that they garnished it better and
cut off the fat. After they turned the corner and were out of my
vision, I looked out across the docks, out to the sea.

Some of the fishing boats were already out working. I could see
them out there, heading out to sea, drifting into the vast expanse.
For a moment all was quiet, and my mind flashed to my previous life
in the city, years ago. For a few seconds I savored the memory of my
former life controlling other people's money. I spent most of what I
made so when I got out of it I didn't take much with me. The trust
account had dried up too, more or less, just about the time that my
family had all died off, except for my sister who was still in Europe,
I think.

A few blocks later I was at the shore and let myself into the beach
house, which I had purchased when I still had a bit of money left
from my old life. The door creaked open and I walked in. For the
past number of years, sixteen or so, I had alternated between living
at the cheaper hotels and the beach house. During the off-season,
hotel rates were cheap and I had maid service, so it was easier to use
the beach house as a studio.

It was cold inside so right away I got down on my knees and built
a fire in the little fireplace. It wasn't much but I had my writing
desk sitting pretty close to it so it warmed me up just fine. I got
the newspaper, the kindling, and a small log together. I stroked the
match and blew on the flame until it was going pretty good. After, I
threw a couple of big ones in there. I sat down and jotted some notes
in my journal.

I always wrote first before I turned my attention to my painting.
It loosened me up and allowed me to get anything paralytic and

negative out before I got my brushes going. Today was the same, and I was able to get quite a bit of work done before taking a long nap around lunchtime.

When I woke up I washed the paint off my fingers and wrists, and then sat on the couch examining a book of matches that I had surreptitiously picked off the floor just inside the front door of the house where we found the dead girl. Normally the sheriff wouldn't have allowed anyone to go into a crime scene like this, but I had lived in town a long time and was the one who reported it. Two weeks of drawn blinds and accumulating papers had caught my eye, so I had been invited to the front door.

After we had seen the dead girl on the floor the sheriff had instructed me to leave, so I don't know what else he might've seen; I was fortunate enough to have grabbed the matchbook, which had the insignia of a club in Albuquerque, New Mexico. It was the "67 Jazz Club" just off Route 66 at exit 6 and had a phone number that someone had scratched in it, in pencil. I spent the rest of the month painting and writing before closing up the shutters in my studio, heading west to the desert. I had been able to grab a newspaper with her picture on it.

I later showed the picture to folks at the "67 Club" and they confirmed it was her. It looked like Rachel, who had only that summer rented the house on the Island. I hadn't run into there during the short spats of time she had been there that season, but I did recognize her from the old days.

Evidently, she'd bought the restaurant from the family who'd owned a bunch of them all over the west. During a drive from Florida to California she'd stopped there for breakfast and found out they were going out of business because the original owners were dying off. She'd gotten the money for it left over from a family inheritance and wanted to go somewhere where she'd never run into anyone from her old life so this had seemed like a good idea.

It was on Route 66 in New Mexico just before the turnoff to go south, just before the Malpais on the western side. This was where

the volcanic ash was sharp and pointed and hurt your feet if you
didn't have good boots. It was right between the few cars that had
come from somewhere else and the southern cactus desert that was
lonely and inhospitable — a good place to hide if you wanted to.

After she'd bought the old diner, the plan was to put the past in
the past and move forward without the moral and karmic inertia to
which her old life had chained her. Free from New England as well
as the European debauchery, she considered that she might actually
make a go of her own life on her own terms.

The girl who had been found on the Island had not been murdered;
she'd been stolen from the entrance to a morgue in New Jersey
and carefully rushed into the trunk of Rachel's car and later onto
the ferryboat. The plan had been hatched in a half-hearted attempt
to fake Rachel's — her own — death. With all the identification
lying around the summerhouse and the deceptive suicide note,
she thought no one would bother to do a DNA analysis and that
everyone would conclude it had been her — Rachel — who had died.
She hoped that news would get back to the City that she had died
and that would be the end of it.

As it later turned out, the family trustee had gotten wind of the
matter, which caused a problem for him. He had sometime learned
that there had been additional monies coming to Rachel and
therefore had to determine what to do with them. After I called him
from the Island in late August, we both agreed that a trip to the
southwest might be in order. Moreover, I was on my way to the west
coast for the winter so the "67" would be right on the way.

The "67" was an Albuquerque jazz club that emulated some of the
goings on in the California cities. Drinks were pricey and the music
contemporary; because it was not a bastion of the American jazz
scene, it had to import musicians from L.A. and New York, Atlanta
and Chicago sometimes. A lot of people had met there; people who
were passing through from one life to another, spending various
amounts of time in the area depending upon the degree to which the
land had enchanted them.

Chapter 4

After the plane touched down I took a cab to the main drag and got
a decent room near the 67 Club. I was on the 4th floor, just above
the fray so I felt safe enough. I was too old to stay on the street
with all the hookers, hustlers, and drug users this poor town had
spawned. My plan was to hang around for a few days or until I got
some answers about the matchbook and the picture.

The owner of the motel was fat and old, resigned to dying at her
post. But this made her confident in her wheelhouse. She said, you
can't bring anyone up to your room without paying extra. When I
looked at her quizzically she realized that I was from out of town and
was not looking for a room for drugs or a hooker. Her look softened
and she asked, without prying, where are you coming from?

I said, I'm from the east. I am looking for the 67 Club — heading
west. She replied by nodding toward the sinking sun in the western
sky, saying: it's over there. I thanked her, went to my room and
slept. When I got up it was later in the evening, dark, and I heard
voices outside in the corridor. I went into the bathroom and looked
into the mirror, pausing for a moment to consider what I was doing.
I was doing research and was trying to put the pieces together about
a serial killer who had died several years ago. I was also trying to
figure out what happened to Rachel.

The motel manager pointed again to the 67 as I headed out of her
office. I noticed in her expressive, leathery face the many layers
of a life long lived, and I wondered what sort of folks drifted into
the desert here. I don't think they were the same sort as the escape
artists who ended up in Alaska even though they all wanted to be
outlanders.

I wandered into the 67 just before the third set, had a couple of
drinks and befriended the bartender. After I gained his trust, I
showed him the pictures I had of the woman who had fled the
Island. He was a bit hesitant at first but when I slipped him a fifty

for my drink he shared that she had been through here a few times, mentioning that she was going to buy a restaurant near the turn off to the Malpais, a good three hours west. I assured him that she was not a fugitive but that I needed to interview her. Head west, he said.

After I finished my drink, I listened to the desert jazz music that was highly influenced by the Spanish culture in the area, and got back to the motel by midnight. The motel woman watched me carefully, and asked me if I had found what I was looking for. I smiled a bit but did not respond, and left in the morning after I drank a Styrofoam cup of black coffee. I headed west on Route 66, slowly, until I could see it from the interstate.

You could see the place from the main highway even though it set back quite a ways on the other side of the old road. It was in New Mexico on Route 66 and was remote. Most days you could drive for a while before you'd see another car. Without the sign just before the turnoff you wouldn't know there was a restaurant there until you were just past it.

She had bought "The Blue Pearl" with a down payment that came from the sale of a string of rare blue pearls she'd gotten in the mail anonymously, along with other family monies leftover. She'd taken the old sign off the building when the owners died and sold their chain. Then she'd gotten a new sign from the city several hours away and had attached it to the front of the building with the help of a couple of guys traveling to California.

Today, she looked out from the double-paned front windows and could tell that it was going to rain soon. It was gray and no direct sunlight fell onto the black and white checkered floor vinyl.

Everyone had left except for a trucker sitting at the counter and a younger couple at one of the front booths.

Anyone want any more coffee? she asked, holding the nearly empty carafe as she leaned toward the kitchen. No, the counter man said. The couple didn't even notice. She elbowed her way past the double doors and poured the rest of the coffee out.

The clock face was at 2:40 p.m. with just less than three hours to go before the evening girl came to relieve her.

She came back out to the counter area and shuffled through the pages of the daily newspaper. There was the front-page story about violence in the Middle East, and several local pieces about the county fair, an investment advisor in the city who had stolen money, and a well-known rancher who had died last week.

It was quiet except for the chatter of the couple. She got up, re-folded the paper, and looked for something to do.

He'd be coming today or tomorrow—she wasn't sure—but she was looking forward to it. Ever since he had first come through town a couple of years ago, she had enjoyed talking with him about what was going on back on the east coast. It was also the case that he was the only one who could get the rest of the money to her.

She looked outside again and heard the light spatter of raindrops. The trucker and the couple paid their bills and left and then there was nothing except for the gray and the rain. She turned on the old radio to country-western music and waited.

She waited a long time and stared out the window. There were no birds here looking back in on her, except for the lone hawk that circled the sagebrush encampment next to the turnoff south just a few miles from the Malpais. She finished sweeping the floor, turned the lights out, and went upstairs to fall asleep in the small apartment on the second floor.

Chapter 5

I packed up the rest of my things and put them on the floor of the passenger side of the Chevy truck, including the amulet I had made from his ashes. Then I headed north along the coast. I had always wanted to do this, be on the road in a truck up the coast, and then back down. Back and forth. Thank God I decided not to wait any longer.

After my father died, I felt compelled to stick around my hometown for a time, putting a rest to all the ghosts of my past. It was, to me, as if my memories were about someone else with my name. That was up north. Then I headed down to California where I had a place, which I sold. I bought the old Chevy, sold everything, and decided to drive up and down the coast. I didn't have a girlfriend at the time, and my children had all moved out east, so I was virtually alone. I got letters from time to time from my old friends, but they had moved on to other relationships and lives and struggles.

Of course, I still had my memories about the old days, but I was losing the point of staying attached. It started to occur to me that I wasn't the same person now as I was then, that the memories were just like a canister of stored films. The fact that I could watch myself with a point of view proved it to me that I was someone else now. All the things I had thought that I wanted had come and gone.

Attach. Enjoy. Detach. Attach. Enjoy. Detach. They were all in service of some goal that seemed to change in form and content as I went along. For now then, I was just going to drive up and down the coast without any goal other than to drive, eat cheap tacos, take in some sun, and drive. This free ontological space was what I had needed for so long, and I was going to enjoy it. Nihilations were inconsequential.

After I got through the hoards of people and the congestion of cars, I ended up in a small town, not even a town really, but a village with cheap hotels and good tacos. It was here that I started what would become this long-term habit of driving up and down the coast with the money I had left from my life savings.

The sun was going down. It was warm. There was a smell of the salt air, meat frying, and beer. I ordered all three and sat under a canopy at the beach, happy with my decision to let go of everything. I had no idea where I was going but I was happy to be free of the attachments.

The last several years had been bizarre. Trying to fit in with the bourgeois had proved a hopeless failure, a farce, and a comedy of errors. It had also been stressful, especially extricating myself from the Island, which I did right before I spent the time up north saying goodbye to the memories.

The dream hadn't come back for while, something for which I was grateful. All that strange shit about Lyken and Dr. Black had really freaked me out but when my therapist and I had finally figured out that it was a self-rendezvous in an interstitial corridor, I started to feel better.

However, this uncovering led to some deeper puzzle that involved fragments of the sun and indigo light that intertwined with all my thoughts, all the time.

I remember the cheap yellow paint in the kitchen, and the way it mixed with the sunlight that streamed through in the mornings, after my Dad had gone to work. I was fully conscious then, almost like an adult in a child's body with a child's identity. Yet, I was fully conscious.

I felt like something was being taken away from me—cumulatively and slowly—during those months and those years, but of course I had no perspective on it. It was almost gothic in a yellow-paint sort of way. There was quietude, a zone of pure silence that would meet up with the baby crying, the phone ringing, and the cheap little television blaring soap operas throughout the morning and the early afternoon.

I was imprisoned. I was captive to a life that I had not chosen, but which had been chosen by me. I suppose that one could construct some sort of spiritual or religious meaning to this but I couldn't see it. Perhaps that is why one day I had wandered down to the railroad tracks, looking left and looking right, but not seeing anything. I couldn't see anything except a vast ontological field of unrefined possibility. It was a way out!

My father's gestures were perfunctory, and he did the best he could with whatever little time he had. Unfortunately, this left me with the yellow paint and the occasional sunbeam that would stream in through the kitchen window. The sunbeam was the same hope as the railroad tracks which, incidentally, were taken away from me after they caught me down there the first time. So, although it gave me great relief when he'd come home at night, every day became heavier than the previous.

I thought about all these things as I drove up and down the coast eating cheap tacos and drinking cold beer on the beach, weighing my options and feeling more liberated than ever.

I reflected on the yellow paint and the sun and the railroad tracks, and I couldn't help but wonder two things: 1) How I was going to resolve the fact that I had been chasing the false self that I had substituted in for the real one, when I was a little boy, and that this had only served to put me off course continuously; and 2) What my life would have been like had I not been forced to trade off what was most real and precious in me at such a young age.

I recognized for the first time ever that this substitution had nearly crushed me and that I knew all along that something wasn't right but didn't know how to fix it. I still wasn't sure what to do it about it. What I did have, however, was the driving up and down the coast and the feeling of freedom.

After several months of my exploring the beach and the driving and the liberation, one night I settled on a cheap hotel somewhere below the Bay and the southern congestion. As the sun dipped down into the water, I ordered a bottled beer and a bit of Mexican dinner.

I noticed the indigo color long before she spoke to me — I could see
it out of the corner of my eye as she roved the tables. I saw how the
indigo fit to her neck and was immediately drawn.

She could see me looking at her necklace with the one indigo-blue
pearl on it, so she spoke right up.

My grandma gave it to me, she said. Want to see it? She leaned
forward, suggesting that I touch it, which I did. It was dark blue
in my hand and immediately filled me with a cornucopia of such
profound feelings I simply did not know what to say. She smiled and
got me the beer and tacos.

In that moment — and during the next two hours while I watched
it get dark and heard the beginning of a music set — I oscillated
between the blue of the pearl and the yellow of the kitchen.
The blue-yellow dialectic entranced me. It was matched by my
restlessness.

The next morning, I had a slight headache, and after two cups of
coffee and breakfast, I continued heading north to the redwoods,
where I was planning on staying for a while. I made it through the
Bay midday, which wasn't so bad, and reached my destination as the
afternoon waned.

I like it here where I was, temporarily in a campground where I'd
made a reservation the day before. There were toilets and electricity,
and a small store with firewood and supplies, so I felt okay.

It was that time of the day when the afternoon was petering out and
the evening was taking over. The temperature had dropped a bit so
I got my fire going, cracked open a beer, and set out to write in my
journal, something I'd been doing for a long time. It was the time
that tied together all the other times for me — helped me make sense
out of things.

I'd set up the tent with the Coleman lantern so I could make out
the marks on the page better, but after a bit I became distracted by
others who were camped nearby. A dog came up to my campsite and

looked at me. He was an older German Shepherd. A male. He came right up to the edge of the fire and looked at me.

I held his gaze for a few moments until he bounded off and then was struck with the most intense interplay of yellow-indigo color I'd ever seen. It was bouncing from the moonlight to the fire to the lantern—it reminded me of a time I'd been in New Mexico driving to my land in a remote area in the middle of the state.

This had been a couple of hours out of Albuquerque to the west, almost to the Malpais and then south into the interior. I'd had cherry pie and a coffee at this diner called the Blue Pearl. I'd not forgotten the name because I'd had quite a conversation with the waitress about how she'd ended up there—out there on her own, alone, in the middle of nowhere, except for the truckers and the bikers and the travelers going between the coasts.

I'd been living in New England for some time, but I'd bought some land in the desert on a whim. Right before the turnoff heading south into the hot desert there had been this restaurant, the Blue Pearl—I don't know if it was there anymore—but I'd stopped in the later afternoon and ended chatting for quite some time with the waitress, who turned out to also be the owner.

It wasn't what we talked about that was important, or what I ate or anything like that. It was the afternoon sun streaming through the windows in just the right angle to create an indigo-blue mixture at the point where they hit the dark floor and the red-vinyl of the seat backs in the booths. It was hard to explain, but I do remember the indigo and the yellow and the conversation.

She seemed out of place as if she had escaped from somewhere from where I'd been which, of course, seemed fantastic. But the conversation had been real, and she seemed familiar to me—not like someone I'd known but someone I might have known, someone I would have known had things been a bit different or if I had made a different choice. I don't even remember her name, and after my two weeks down into the desert I didn't stop back at the Blue Pearl again. Instead, I'd headed west and north to take care of some family business.

Anyway, after the German Shepherd bounded off into the darkness, I continued to write. Not only was I putting to pen several personal notes, I was working on a new piece of fiction that I was writing. The working title was long, but it amused me so I kept it: Everyone's Having Such a Good Time (Is this all there is?) The reason I take note of this is that it has always seemed that there was more to things than met the eye just as it seemed that my life would have been different had I not traded what was most real in me to survive the circumstance that had been allotted to me. They were the same sensation, I think, involving a keen awareness of ontological space — the interstitial corridor that is the origin of all things and all changes.

I finished the journal entry and my contributions to the new fiction. I turned the lantern off and, as the fire died down, I could see the medley of orange-red near the outside of the flames, but as you got nearer the inside it was yellow, then blue. Indigo-blue. I checked that my pistol was loaded, got into the tent, and fell asleep to my dreams.

Mr. Lykeman. Please stop trying to move. You've had a major rupture, Mr. Lykeman. Please just lie still.

I tossed and turned all night, going in and out of the dream. Heard the Shepherd padding around the campground. Murmured voices. Then it was total darkness and complete quiet. It was total darkness like I had experienced after leaving my psychotherapy sessions in another town, in another time, so long ago. To explain, let me say that the darkness was both practical and ontological. It was practical because the sessions always ended in the later afternoon just as the sun was going down; ontological because the darkness ran over me like the water did when I was a baby being washed in the bathtub.

I woke to a sliver of sun that had knifed its way into the tent. Cars were pulling out of the campground. The dog had vanished. I was virtually alone until the ranger came by late morning to check on things. I told him I'd be packing up and gone in just a few minutes, to which he assented, the rhythm of our dialogue humdrum, mechanical.

I grabbed a Styrofoam coffee at the store and pulled onto the gravel road that'd lead me back onto the highway where I'd be heading deeper into the forest, east, away from the water. I needed the quiet.

Chapter 6

The "lavatory," as they liked to call it, was always clean. It was super-clean, so fucking clean you could have eaten a meal off the floor. Anyway, you had to wait until break or lunch to go in there regularly; otherwise, you had to ask for permission.

Everything was on a schedule here which made me like a stranger for the whole eight years. I liked nothing about it. I liked nothing about primary school and its ideological indoctrinations and specifications.

I had a girlfriend in first grade and another in third, including Rachel before she left. When I reached seventh and eighth grade, I was a time bomb completely entombed in expectation and protocol. Proper behavior. Homework. Performance. And trips to the lavatory, which at least got me out of class for momentary respite. It was bizarre looking back that the main color other than the gray-white tile floor was kitchen yellow. But there was no indigo here.

Trips to the principal's office and correction, along with the kudos I'd achieved from high grades, had worn into me like a dog collar that you'd forgotten to take off for years. So I did the things I had to do to get the praise and tried like hell to avoid the other. Unfortunately, things weren't always fair, like the time I got paddled for engaging in a snow fight when actually I hadn't engaged at all. But it didn't matter what I said.

My parents didn't know about any of this. Instead, all they looked for was my smile as they waited for me at the bus stop.

The "hunt," as it was called by the locals, was that time of the year when all the school age children went hunting with their Dads. This included the girls, too, and no one thought it strange. But I didn't go and therefore every fall was one of the very few children sitting in class on Opening Day. It was special privileges for the few of us who had bothered to come to school; as such, we could go to the lavatory whenever we wanted, without permission.

Walking through the deserted halls each of those opening days gave me ontological traction, and I was fortunate enough to have been granted several of these privileged experiences even before grade school. Of course, this was paradoxically good and bad, "positive" and "negative" some would say, because I got to experience my "freedom" from the beginning. In later years, I would retrospectively question this so-called freedom, seeing it as possible illusion. But it felt good then, until I lost it.

The worst thing was that I didn't even know that I'd lost it. Over time, being subjected as a child to the ideological oppression of the working class, I lost the ability to distinguish between the "real" and the ideal. Everything was just what it was; it was a way of life that no one person or even a group of philosopher-kings had planned. In order to avoid persecution, jail, shame, or even worse we all just organically moved with the tide and lost the critical space that I'd always thought provided my freedom.

So, I came to relish those days when the others were hunting or off on some other voluntary field trip, instead opting for extra time with my teachers, or spending the afternoon in the library working on a report. Then, as I said, this vision of freedom grew dim and I didn't even realize it.

At first I resisted, calling attention to the irrationalities of the whole program with the expected wit of a seven year old. This set me on a course of being objectified as a troublemaker even though I was always at the top of the class and excelled with ease. That additional fact—one might expect—caused even more of a stir and more resentment because it naturally caused those in charge, and their charges, to re-think the mission of the whole vessel. By now yellow streaks of the kitchen I'd spent my first few years in had left my immediate consciousness, replaced by the antiseptic gray of the boys' lavatory, with yellow trim.

Going home after school in the late afternoon was tedious as well, though I didn't understand it at the time. There'd be false greetings and stressful dinners. More pressure to get in line and "do what's right." So the dialectic became an oscillation between "doing what was right" or getting into trouble. There was no compromise on this. So the false self started growing right alongside the other, and I therefore started walking down on a long road of self-division and fragmentation.

I didn't know it at the time, but all the wear and tear from the back and forth wore a hole in me from which constantly trickled and spilled my dreams, hopes, and desires. Of course, I tried to shore it up with some of the defense mechanisms Freud wrote about, but this only served to create noise, obfuscation, and mental clutter. Everything became complicated, as it were, and I just thought this was normal.

The principle would punish me. Students wouldn't know whether to love me or hate me. My parents became concerned from time to time, but didn't know how to deal with it so the whole thing dragged on and escalated as all matters do.

I guess I had what you call a "chip on my shoulder," which I still don't really understand the meaning of, but I think it has to do with self-esteem or a hole in your heart or something like that. Yet, because of the rigidity of the culture and its protocol for me, I had to engage my resistance in a structure that didn't allow for it without certain costs.

School was easy but monotonous so I hurried myself to the library every chance I got so I could read what I wanted to read and not what some idiot administrative committee thought. Yet with all the sports, the school projects, and the mandatory family events, including church and old people, I had little time for contemplation. This, itself, was oppression, but along with the small-town ideology I was sunk. Moreover, since I wasn't able to take up residence in one self or the other, I really wasn't one at all, except for the mal-organized framework in which I'd find myself when I was in the rage.

Years later, I'd appeared at that same grade school for an event, ended up in the "lavatory" at intermission, and noticed that the walls were still antiseptic gray, along with the yellow strips that some painter had applied as an after thought.

High school was the same. College was the same. More expectations. More structure. More ideology. But when I got the big job offer just after graduation, the financial seduction and the kudos from my family again arrested my motivation to break free, whatever that meant. Whatever that means.

It was an accounting firm and they were going to subsidize my tuition if I wanted to do more schooling. But this required a lot of reports and forms and luncheons, and therefore time away from the road I wasn't even sure I wasn't on. That is, it became apparent — in some unclear way — that I didn't even have the ability to think about what I was doing. I had just been ushered down a certain road, and I was expected to continue with it "because I had so much invested."

My best friend, Rachel, from grade school had moved on with her life even though she called me now and then, strung out on some new guy or some new designer drug. Early on — perhaps 3rd or 4th grade — her family had moved back East when they got the inheritance money. I didn't understand at the time, but I knew that in some important way she was different, and that there would always be an unbridgeable distance between us.

I loved her when we were younger, but I wasn't from the same class and there were all sorts of forces to keep us apart. As I got older, we'd meet up over the holidays, but as the drugs and the stress took a toll on her face, they also diminished the energy between us.

We met a couple of times at her family's summer home on the east coast; a couple of others she paid my way to the Southwest, where we spent a couple of days shacked up in a seedy motel drinking cheap wine, reminiscing about the old days, and me trying to find the her that no longer seemed to be. Since I had never had any equanimity with my own self either I was like a drunken marksman trying to hit a moving target in the wind with a bow that was improperly strung and an arrow that was bent. It was in name only.

Rachel, I think you just have to let it go, I'd say.

I know, she'd mumble, sloshing that red wine down her gullet all the while.

I somehow knew that nothing would ever be the same and that the machinations we went through were not going anywhere, except in that same old tired place I was still in with my own narrative.

After a certain point I quit meeting up with her. Heard that she'd run off to France when her family money ran out, though knowing her she'd probably stashed as much as she could all over the U.S. With her life—running scared—having cash from state to state allowed her to keep on the move.

Meanwhile, my career continued to move forward, even though I questioned whether being an accountant served my college dream of becoming a psychologist. In the meantime, I worked long hours and spent the rest of them with my wife. We'd had a daughter but she died a long time ago.

I knew that I'd always remember that sick yellow paint on the lavatory walls. Every time I'd see something similar I was inexorably pulled into the past. Not only into my early school days, but also into my time on the "Island," as they liked to call it.

Chapter 7

My first job had been with a company called "The Organization."
Since I'd done so well in school I'd received a signing bonus—which
I promptly spent on drinks, clothes, women, and a car—and a
number of perks that were "normal" according to the manager of my
department.

I had my name on a locker at the downtown gym. I had Neiman's
suits. I went to expensive restaurants and bought fancy Chardonnay.
When I wasn't in court, I was in one of those restaurants or at the
firm, either in my office or the conference room. It was business all
the way, and all anyone ever talked about was money. They made
me want that money. More of it. As much of it as I could get. This
value operated as the logic of all our conversations and all of our
work.

My many girlfriends provided me with the sustenance to pursue
my files with zeal and focus. Mergers & Acquisitions. Yet I always
found time early or at lunch to slink off to some dark café to sit
unnoticed as I penned the thoughts I could not say in my real life.

However, I'd always be noticed by the receptionist as I came in to
the office. It was like she had this finely-honed radar for me. She
never could figure out where I'd come in from—didn't ask—didn't
care—but she could drill a gaze right into my marrow.

"Pearl," as she was called, was a pretty brunette from the Midwest
upon whom fortune always smiled. I didn't give a shit about that,
however. I was more interested in her radar, which seemed to
afford her an ability to know what I was thinking or where I'd
been, so the conversation was never a two-way street. What's more,
her commentary was always patronizing, most likely to serve the
interests of our mutual employer, The Organization, whose most
immediate departmental manager was everywhere, in multiple
places at once.

She'd say things like (often looking at her wristwatch):

— —-The meeting's just starting. Better hurry.

— —-Be careful with them (shaking her head disapprovingly;
referring to the cleaning staff in the building whose ranks included
some very beautiful albeit poor women).

— —-You look tired!

I'd always smile, especially because I knew the meta-text was just
there to hide the subtext which, in all reality, was the main text. The
simple truth of the matter was that I sometimes felt like an imposter
and it was her job—she'd been appointed!—to correct me.

Then I'd make my way either to my office or to the conference
room. It went this way day in and day out. The money kept coming
in. I got my promotions. I had a few serious relationships.

Once late afternoon when I was playing hooky from work—having
just left a strip club and on the way home via a jazz club that served
good Chardonnay—I accidentally ran into her. Not that she was
going in to the jazz club. Instead, we literally almost ran into each
other in a shared parking lot, one to the club, the other to a jewelry
store.

She'd been leaning down to pick up some pearls that had fallen off a
string. Tahitian Blues, she'd said. Expensive.

I ran over there to help and afterwards we sat for a few minutes
and talked. Then she gave me one of the blue pearls from the string,
saying that it'd bring me luck. When I walked by her the next day
she acted more professional than ever. Stiff. Almost stiff from rigor.
But we never talked personally again although she continued to say
encouraging things to me when I walked by or when she saw me in
the lunchroom.

After a weekend in the desert sniffing illicit drugs and drinking
without control, I managed to slip by her desk one day, hoping not

to be noticed so that I didn't have to listen to her or say anything. But she wasn't there. I later learned that she had gone off to die of cancer and nobody from the office had said anything. That's the way it was done in The Organization. There was a new girl forthwith.

Later in the week, it must have been Saturday, I was busy at home doing some "creative" writing, which I engaged in more often than not to overcome the monotony of my life away from the Organization. In fact, I was so committed to my job that I rarely considered other forms of life experience, except for the writing and the edgy, dark cafes I frequented.

Chapter 8

There was a spider crawling down from the windowsill. I figured in about five minutes he'd make it inside so I closed it up. Even with the fan on high it'd soon be hard to breathe in here, but I figured I could get a page or two out beforehand. Sure enough that spider had gone all the way down to the opening hoping it'd be open and I was sure that he'd been inside before. Meanwhile I let the sunshine spill in through the dirty window, hoping that he'd just go away.

I'd been pondering something all week and by Friday it'd come to me like black crows on snow: This insatiable, ineluctable drive away from the hole in Being was futile. We all had it, and it always had us.

There was never any closure for more than a moment. It's like no matter what you did or what you thought, there was this cosmic sliver that cut like a knife through whatever you thought you'd done. It was a sort of rupture that was always happening—like sweeping a floor clean and while putting the broom in the closet noticing a piece of dirt on it. I chased these breaks just like anyone else, but I'd always thought that there must be a way out of it.

I was so busy at work that by the time Friday rolled around and I'd had dinner, I had just enough energy for a beer and then sleep. During the weekend, I literally had nothing to do except for the mundane: movies, new restaurants, maybe the gym for a few pushups and steam. But one day I met a gal in a café where I was drinking coffee and reading one of the local rags that came out with titillating advertisements.

She was writing—seemed totally into it and I didn't want to bother her but she noticed that I dropped a book on the ground and picked it up for me. Her name was Raven and she was a graduate student in literature or something like that. Long story short, we spent a few nights together until it burned out, but I took from it a passion for the mysteries of writing. She had encouraged mine but would never know it.

Her words: I think I can find him if I look long enough. I think
I can figure it out if I think enough. I think I can understand if I
contemplate in the right way.

Thus is the problem of modernity, but she was resolute, which
I admired, and besides, her name triggered several nights to the
public library, checking out book after book about the raven.

It wasn't about the girl at all. It was, however, about the rupture
she caused in me. After a few conversations with her we never
spoke again, even though she had ignited in me a new horizon of
possibilities.

For a time, my series of encounters with the girl acted only to
squelch my desire to think about my life. I threw myself into my
work with an intensity I'd never known before, coming to the office
early, staying late, and generally becoming a top performer. I'd
gotten another promotion with my name on the door and I newly-
found sense of respect.

What do you think about this, Mr. Lykeman? I'd hear often.

Meetings would never start without me.

I got specialized license plates.

My bank account grew along with my self-esteem.

One day, accidentally, I was coming back from a meeting and
impulsively decided to pull over at a park and go for a walk. It was
warm out, just a few clouds in the air, so I put my jacket on the seat
and went walking in the park.

I'd never been here before even though I'd driven by it perhaps
thousands of times. It was small and had a trail that went around the
whole place. It was a dirt trail, well-worn, and there were only a few
people around so I didn't feel crowded.

It was bizarre for me to stray off my main route. I had the logic all figured out and it was clearly working for me. However, something about the yellow car that I could see pulling up behind my car and the sorrowful woman sitting on the bench pulled at me.

I noticed her midway around primarily because she was alone but mostly because her face was pointed downward into the grass directly in front of her. I walked around twice and both times tried to get her attention.

The second time she glanced up at me and I smiled but not invasively. She immediately looked down and I made my way back to my office. There was a small raven—perhaps a crow — looking at me on my way out of the park. He cawed once and flew away.

Back at the office, past the new receptionist, safely ensconced in my files, mid-afternoon I shut my door and closed my blinds. Then I just sat. I thought about the woman at the park, her apparent sadness, and the crow on the way out. I recall reading a book back in college called "Ravenswood." It was about a doctor who had murdered one of his patients. My girlfriend from the early days, interestingly enough, Rachel, had been raised there after she left my town.

I sat motionless for a time, careful not to move lest I interrupt the golden-yellow sunbeam making its way through the window and across the carpet. That's when I started formulating my plan.

I needed to get out but I was so embedded in my world that I had no perspective, so I didn't really even understand what "Out" meant. I did know that I didn't want to be here in my office of The Organization so I left and drove home to see my parents who wouldn't be pleased no matter what I did.

You're thinking of quitting your job!

You've put so much time into it. That doesn't make any sense.

What will you do?

Dinner was served and uneventful. My father, as usual, didn't have much to say other than a few gruff remarks and the comments about dinner. Then he went out into his work shed and that was it. I few more empty comments by my mother had me wondering why I'd even driven out to the country to see them.

I left, still formulating my plan.

Chapter 9

I woke up still thinking of the raven on the windowsill. I drank a coffee and sat in the living room looking at the mantel. I closed my eyes for a moment, getting ready for my morning nap, which would take me to lunch. Instead, I had an impulse to call the company doctor, who had been contacting me regularly as to my progress.

I called him on the telephone.

Yes, Mr. Lykeman, everything will be fine.

Okay, Doctor, I think I can.

Today?

Okay. I will see you this afternoon in your office.

I put the telephone down and sat in my kitchen with the yellow walls that accented the fading French blue. It was difficult for me to stay right in the here and now. I kept fading out to some unknown point in time in the past.

I put my head down while sitting at the kitchen table and started nodding out. Then I woke — I'm unsure of how much time passed — and my head was throbbing. I closed my eyes and saw blood streaming down my forehead and the pain was intense and cutting. My head really hurt. I got up, ate some aspirin, and took a shower.

I felt my forehead and it still hurt. It had been this way for a long time, but had been getting worse over the past year. The company doctor said it was stress and nothing more, but I felt like a whole lifetime was caught up in those headaches.

I found one of my best suits, combed my hair, and carefully nosed my Mercedes downtown to the underground parking stall. Took the elevator. Walked down the long hallway to the company suite, and made it to my office. Nobody looked up as I passed down the hallway, I guess because they were all expecting me to show up eventually. No one really left here except when they expired.

For the next hour I worked diligently and was perfunctory in my speech and mannerisms. I quickly caught up on some basic scheduling and at the appointed time, went to another floor to see the doctor for my medication. There were two bottles, and he assured me that if I took the pills as suggested I would feel better soon, perhaps within two weeks.

I complied, and stayed at the office later than usual, starting the catch up process so I could be back in the swing of things. I was generally regarded as one of the Organization's best employees, so I suppose everyone was silently rooting for me to come back and be better than ever. Even with the rupture, I'm sure they all believed that I'd come back to be even more productive.

It went like this for a couple of weeks until the medication started working and by then I was just numb again. I was back to my managerial position even though I could still not bring myself to look at —- to confront — my rupture. The company doctor, of course, encouraged me in his affable way, but I wasn't ready. I did know that when I did inspect the rupture, I'd do it in the privacy of my own home.

Eventually I apologized to the Vice-President I'd attacked in the hall before the doctor sedated me.

—I'm so sorry, I said. Please forgive me.

—It's just fine, she replied. Everything will be okay. In her generosity she quickly proved why she had a more senior position than me.

She was stronger.

Anyway, with the chemicals running around in my brain, I was back into position in no time. On occasion, I'd eat my lunch at the park where I ran into the woman from time to time. She was married and it wasn't a budding affair. However, I did learn that she was very sick and went to chemotherapy for her cancer.

She invited to me to come to her group where sick people talked with each other about their sickness. Since I'd had a major rupture, I would be welcome with open arms. {My guess was that everyone would want to talk to her about my condition, comparing it with his or her own.]

One day, I went to a meeting with the sick people — with the other sick people — and we spoke about our mixed feelings. Some thought we were just more sensitive than the others. But in any case, I left with the mixed feelings, went home and sat in my living room looking at the mantel and hearing two days worth of scratching at the kitchen window until I got up and saw the raven hanging out at the windowsill, just above where the yellow paint became white around the sill.

Chapter 10

My experience on the Island was where I was most tested so far in my life. I was lucky to have escaped from it alive and with my soul intact. It was where I'd spent a few years right before I tied up my father's affairs and took the truck down to southern California, on the coast.

Things are never just what they seem at that time, being capable of an infinite number of temporal and interpretational constructions, depending upon your mood at the time. This was never truer than in affairs of the heart, matters that had taken me to distant shores and to the anguish of human emptiness, and to misery. With her it was wretched misery, like scratching at the walls of the Château D'If.

The worst of it was that I knew I was in prison from the first day, that I'd been caught in a spider's web and that there was no way out. I later realized that, like all things, the web itself would implode upon itself, move, or be torn to shreds by the wind or the storms of time.

This is not working me, I'd say.

She'd say, you knew. I told you.

But then we'd continue in this loop that went on and on, exhausting us both beyond measure. I think, in retrospect, that the mutual torment gave us something to cling onto instead of the ontological freedom that was worse: its beckoning had been terrifying!

But I received an experiential lesson in the life of the bourgeois like I never could have otherwise. Everything was stratified: which street you lived on, where you shopped, where you vacationed, where you sent your kids to school. What was even more noticeable was the branding.

"Branding," as I used to say, involved choice in consumer goods.

Regular shoes would never do. Instead, you had to put a buckle here
and an extra button there. Anything that did not have extra flash
and bling was automatically rejected as boring. What was actually
being communicated was that they needed a way to differentiate
themselves from the great unwashed, from the hoi polloi.

Money itself meant little; it was this differentiation mechanism that
was important. For example, once I accidentally ran into a soccer
Dad who had just gotten off work to pick up his daughters. He was
dressed in a tailored suit and I was in jeans and a t-shirt. I noticed
him looking me up and down, codifying me into a lesser class
citizen. He couldn't have possibly been interested in what I was
doing with my life.

I noticed, however, even though the rich and the very rich
occasionally bumped into each other at one of the local pizza joints,
they still had their separating-differentiating looks. At the time, I was
still a member of the proletariat, so I couldn't even enter into these
exchanges. All the same, it felt no different than spending a weekend
camping in the Malpais, in New Mexico: dry, barren, alone.

I had to get the fuck out of there. I said that so many times I was
dizzy and nauseous about it. Still, I stayed for a while, muscling
my way through the carnival of consumerism that had imploded on
itself.

No, those shoes are all wrong.

Shit, my car doesn't have the right little metal sign. I have to get
another [car].

You only belong to three clubs?

There's always Palm Springs if the Paris trip doesn't work out.

You must get a real job.

The dry wind of the Malpais scorched my throat, more when I
was on the Island than when I was actually there. Then, to add

salty insult, I discovered one day that there was another island and another set of codes. And more alienation

And separation-differentiation. And the Islands fought for the most "Island" status, which revolved around the fatness of the wallets and the size of the homes. These considerations led to the greatest amount of distancing between people, a goal most of the affluent strived for openly.

Still, I stayed, pretending to enjoy the implosion that had stripped me of my freedom, my decency, and my esteem. In fact, I had so neatly imprisoned myself that I almost forgot the escape hatch that I had constructed at the beginning.

The Malpais cut hard on your feet even if you wore the rough and tough hiking boots from the expert-class hiking boot store. It was the devil's backyard. The sun burned into your eyes, the ground into your feet, and there was no direction anywhere. Thus, you had to navigate by the cairns, reaching one and looking for the next, squinting in the sun to find each pile of rocks so you could get out of there lest you lose yourself in the desert. Even then, it was touch and go to get back to the car.

The underground cave was pitch-black but cool because it was totally away from the sun. You couldn't see anything. When the last flashlight started flickering, I knew it was time to get the hell out of there so I moved fast, even falling a couple of times to head for what I thought was the speck of light.

The light grew larger and eventually I made it back to the blinding sun that cut through me like the sharp rock that was left over from the meteor. Life on the Island was just like the Malpais. It cut through me hard, so blinding in fact that I vacillated between the sun and the cave, in a perpetual ironic state of ambiguity.

For some odd reason, though, I kept a trace of my escape plan deep inside me from the beginning.

I could feel the implosion impinging hard down on me everyday,

sucking the life out of me, forcing me to comply, forcing me
to become one of them, which I could never do. As such, I did
not fit. As such, I was marginalized as "bad" or "evil" in some
way, ostracized [though it was subtle in this culture], and even
encouraged to take part in the implosion.

Sick and wretched I moved forward, realizing that my thought
experiment was getting the better of me, coming to grips with the
hot sun and the dark cave.

Flashes of my condo on the California coast would flash before
my eyes. Memories of my childhood on the east coast would
penetrate me as well, but seemed mostly like pictures from a book I
remembered in a half-sort of way.

The raven scratched at the windowsill, and still I could not figure
out who had killed the girl on Falcon Island, back in the east. But
I would always remember the yellow from the bathroom and the
way that woman from the park would look at me. I always intended
on returning to the Malpais one day, perhaps on my way back to
Florida, if it ever got that far.

I was the most dangerous game! By the time I finally realized that
she was a collector, and I was just the most recent, all the damage
had been done. My ideological naivety had been preyed on, but
it was a big lesson about living in your own classist narcissism, a
mistake I'd never make again.

On the other side of things, I imagine her frustration in never being
able to conquer my freedom. As Freud would have it that which
cannot be expressed in consciousness [presumably in the light with
transparency] migrates into the unconscious [presumably the dark
with murky lines]. So she was unfulfilled and I barely escaped with
my dignity.

Sometimes the wind blows us to places we'd never go otherwise;
we're there at the door being inveigled; all intuition says to run for
the hills; still, we peer in, hoping to see something that might take
away the numbing and the logic of the life we know.

So we enter and cut our feet. On occasion it is so bad that it ends up killing us over it when all we really had to do was to flee, just like Rachel did to The Blue Pearl Restaurant in a remote region in western New Mexico near the Malpais.

I still had not been able to figure out who the dead girl was—yet—but I would eventually. In the meantime, I made several trips back from the Pacific Northwest or from California to camp south of the Malpais. I'd always stop at the Blue Pearl and talk to the owner.

Chapter 11

I'd started going to the park nearly everyday, especially when I found out that she was sick. She'd be there—her face pale, her body thin, he face sad. She was a wisp of nothingness, I thought, gloomy and self effacing, facing a gloomy and inert park that seemed like a morgue.

That's it, a morgue! I'd been to this park before, under different circumstances and in a different time, and it'd been different, with more natural light and with a softer feel. Here, now, though, it was strangely black and she was there, too, dressed in dark, her face partially covered.

Though it was heavy in the park in a weird sort of way, it was a pleasant repose from the apathy, the transitory passion, and the narcissism of what appeared otherwise and elsewhere. It was almost like a graveyard, a necropolis of nothingness that seemed more or a dream than anything else.

One day I followed her out of the park along the sidewalk until she went into a building that housed a number of professionals. I watched closely until she knocked on a door with the name "Dr. Strangell" on it. I saw his hand reach out for her and then the door closed.

For some time then I would watch her in the park and sometimes I'd follow her to that building. A couple of times I passed her while she was sitting on a bench in the park and I thought she was looking at me.

She would look up and as if on cue I would immediately look down. The only exception to this was one day something fell from her hand onto the pathway in front of the bench. I picked it up and gave it to her. She thanked me, smiling in a self-effacing sort of way. I noticed it was a picture so I asked her about it.

That's Rachel, she said.

Oh, your daughter.

Yes, she said, my daughter. Then she was quiet and I left.

I would recall for weeks after that exchange how the lines at the
corners of her eyes became sharp and pronounced, vigilant and
attentive — there was a cutting sadness that I could see there so I
didn't say anything.

Within two months of these fragmented meetings we were sitting on
the park benches together sharing personal details about our lives.

She had cancer. She said that she had been this way for most of her
life but that recently she'd had a diagnosis, which was that she was
"gravely ill" and without chemotherapy would most likely die soon.
In return, I explained about my "rupture" and that I was trying to
regain my health as well. This led to her sharing about the support
group which I soon joined.

The group itself was comprised of all sorts of individuals suffering
from various diseases. We'd sit and look at each other, drink black
coffee from Styrofoam, and share our mutual malaise. Of course,
I was always excited to see Milena there and particularly enjoyed
our fifteen-minute breaks when we could walk outside and speak
personally for a few moments.

I told them that I'd had a major rupture in my life and that I'd had
to take off some time for work, to which they all nodded their heads
knowingly. I shared about my big job as an accountant but that a
long time ago I'd hoped to be an investigator, privately interested in
forensic psychology. I explained that because I wasn't interested in
the uncertainty of it, I'd chosen a more certain career in numbers.

Someone suggested I get into psychotherapy and gave me a business
card of a psychoanalyst who was good. Dr. Black was his name
and I called him later in the week. After a good conversation he
referred me to a Dr. Strangell, with whom I met in a well-appointed,
downtown therapist's office.

It wasn't the first time I'd been in therapy, but it was the first time
I had played at it. I was more interested in the Doctor himself and
what he did to heal people. I fed him a story about neglectful and
somewhat abusive parents, feigned all the right non-verbal gestures,
and generally did my part in the two-person theatre. I asked him
about a picture of his wife on his desk—which he did not answer—
and we got off to a good start.

By the time 45 minutes passed and I wrote the check, I'd always be
ready to get back to work at the Organization. A series of walks,
a cab, and a bus, and I'd be back to my office on my floor in my
building on my street. Who was the savage here, anyway? Was it
me, myself, or the healer?

Was it the natural beast who just lived or the "civilized man" who
was the savage? No longer sure, and completely unraveling even
with the medicine the company doctor was giving me, I was haunted
by memories of a better time. A more creative time.

One day after speaking with her in the park, I hurried back to
the office on foot but was distracted by the dark blue iridescence
that I noticed in my peripheral vision as I passed the cemetery. At
first he just hopped along from tree branch to sidewalk to bush,
looking at me, cocking his head left to right, and then staring. Then
he appeared right in front of me—it must have been twenty paces
away.

I stopped and looked at him while he looked at me. I realized that I
no longer needed to be in the golden sunlight of my kitchen with the
yellow paint to have an encounter with him. We just stared, the big
raven and I. Then I crumpled to the concrete and everything went
dark again.

The mumbling voices had no impact on me. My head hurt and I
could smell east coast fish. My mouth was dry like a day in the
Malpais. I could feel the garotte tighten. I could see the blade slice.
I could see my father planting potatoes, on his knees in the garden. I
could recall my first cigarette and my first touch between her legs.

Mr. Lykeman, she said. Look at me, Mr. Lykeman. You're going to be okay. Then everything felt calm, like soaking in hot springs or lying in a warm bed. I swear I could see that blue iridescence all the way to the hospital. Later, the Organization Doctor came to see me and prescribed a stronger dose of medication. You'll be all right now, he said. I can sense it. You just had to get rid of some negative energy.

Chapter 12

If I were really honest with myself and not so concerned with whether I was virtuous or not, I'd have to admit that I despised my psychotherapist for at least two reasons. I didn't like how he treated his wife, nor did I like his subtle, false modesty. It was contemptuous, and disconnected to my reality, especially in the way that he used words that fell out of my ambit.

I wanted to kill him, to be sure, and I did have fantasies about rescuing his bride. Instead, though, I took a break from therapy, talked to the raven at my kitchen window, and then took a trip back to the east coast.

Is that you? she said, when I picked up the receiver. Is that you?

Yes, I replied. I'm back. (Back on Island where the girl had been murdered the prior summer.)

Good, she said. Come by the diner sometime and get a bowl of chili—on me.

I replied that I had to take care of some business for a couple of days, that I'd be off to the mainland and up the cost by train to do some legal business. Then, when I got back from Crowville, I'd stop by for that chili later in the week.

I headed up north, up the coast where it was colder the farther you went. It was cold up here, and I figured this'd be one of the last times. After a combination of the boat, the train, and a rental car, I headed through the snow [it was early winter]. When I got there the old man was exactly where I'd left him, sitting in front of the fireplace sipping coffee and writing in his journals. He'd heard me drive up, but he never came to the door so I just let myself in.

He nodded to the kitchen and I fixed us some lunch. Then we talked. We talked as we always did, both of us making pithy philosophical comments about the work until we tired. Then we'd finish with some religion and politics, say a few things about the family, and then we were done.

It was on the outskirts of a small town off the main highway. It was away from the people who drove to the coast up here when it was warm, and we were essentially alone. I knew that there were a few others who brought him supplies so it wasn't anything to concern myself with; besides, he'd always had things his way and I knew he could move if he wanted to.

I took a walk around the place and then down to the water, noticing the sun that was poking out from the clouds. This up here had all been a path I could have taken but didn't. It had become a mere loose end that I had to tie up, and I wouldn't be coming back anymore even though I had said the same thing the past several years.

The ravens were out. They were out watching me and I could see this through the golden yellow filter of the thin stream of sunlight that was glinting from above. They were having a convention of sorts, engaged in some complicated dialectic about an obvious unsolved political issue. My presence interrupted them so they took a break and sat watching me. They watched me watching them. I sat this way for a long time in the silence except for the small lapping of the little waves dancing into shore. I was alone except for them. I was alone.

After what little afternoon sun there was started to wane, I got up from my perch on the small wooden pier and walked back to his house.

There, I gathered the legal papers, finished another half cup of coffee, and said goodbye to him. I knew this would be the last time. I could feel it in his handshake. I looked into his eyes. We embraced. For just a moment we could both sense the letting-go part of the respective roles we had played for many years. He would soon be entering the Netherland and I would be wrapping up other matters so I could get back to the other side — making my way to the rivers.

I shook his hand more vigorously as I pushed the front door open.
There was maybe a small tear forming in the pocket between the
inside of his eye and the soft, aged flesh around it. But he didn't let
the tear out. Instead, he kept it in as always and I pushed the door
open. I let go of his hand—and of him—of all the anger I'd about
it all that had held me back my whole life. I was letting it go and as
I walked out onto the porch the sun winked at me, a nice, bright
yellow smile just like I had experienced when I emerged out of the
dark-black cave in the Malpais, near The Blue Pearl Restaurant.

It was like an orgasm in a way. Enter through the door in one
mood and exit in another. Move from one dimension to the next,
punctuated by a series of "little deaths" that intensified through time
for me. I got into my car, the sun still winking, and looked through
the kitchen window. I looked up through the kitchen window
through which the golden life of the sun was streaming its joy and
its agony and I could see him looking back at me. He was crying. I
knew then that I'd never see him again, and that in time I'd forget
about it and in time that it would not matter anymore.

I let my eyes adjust to the sun up here in the north just like I did
when I was out in the desert. Like He had this place out here I had
my own deep into the Netherworld south of the Malpais where the
Outlanders lived. I'd gone down there may years ago, in a quite
unexpected way, taking an unexpected job and an unexpected
assignment that ended up not so far away from the border. Thus,
my time down there—below the sharp rock—had been unexpected
but had also brought the fortuitous gift of cheap land and a place to
collect my thoughts. It was the unparalleled solitude that I needed.

I drove south along the eastern coast to the ferry. By the time I got
to the Island, it was early evening so I headed straight to the beach
house. I emptied most of my duffel bags into the drawers, had a
drink, and sat outside on the deck to watch the sun set and listen to
the waves rhythmically dancing their way in.

The waves danced to a rhythm that reminded me of the way the
wind would sweep over the meadows and hills of the valley where
I had grown up. It was a steady, natural rhythm that always led

me to peace—and to freedom from the worries that life brought. These waves here pushed up against the sandy beach in a gentle but probing way, which soon put me into a meditative stupor.

The combination of the trip up north, the drink, and the long day had made me tired; as the sun set in the west and started to slowly sink downward into the belly of the earth, I lost consciousness. I was dimly aware of this but welcomed it. I welcomed the portal to my sleep, which I knew would deliver me to the other universes I inhabited.

I watched him greet his wife and kiss her. It was repugnant to me because I knew that he could never know her as I did. Let me be clear that this was not an affair that I was referring to; instead, it was a conjunction of two souls who may or may not have known each other in the past, but two souls who understood each other deeply. No practical mundane relationship could ever penetrate that depth.

I understood this especially when I was in the park—that darkened park that filled me with such morose sadness. There was a shadow cast there that was so tragic, a force that pulled me in to a counter-memory that threatened my sanity. When Dr. Black referred me to him, I wholly believed that he could help me, even though I despised the bourgeois nature of their relationship.

I grew to enjoy the stillness of the park as I later did the necropolis situated only a few blocks away. I went there for contemplation and to see her. I later joined a support group she was in with the wayward people who had broken away from the what-it-was, and who no longer fancied themselves the bourgeois. All was lost here in this tragic and dark existential separation.

I woke up in the middle of the night to the waves and the moon. I picked myself up just enough to flop down onto the bed before I passed out again.

I fell fast asleep to my dreams again.

This time, I re-emerged in a cemetery. It seemed like I had been here before. It was very old with overgrown weeds and gravestones that were hard to read. The moon was there, lighting my way as I walked deeper into the darkness.

I remember wanting to take his life but I lacked the will. I felt the rage and the resentment. I had the intellect and I had the opportunity. Yet I lacked a sufficient drive to carry out my plan. So much I had wanted to put an end to his terrible nature but every time my plan became concrete enough to execute, I had engaged in a mind trick so that it wouldn't happen. Instead, the bad conscience grew inside me to enormous proportions, spilling out from me in every conceivable direction.

I lost a lot of sleep those days, going back and forth from my nice home to my quiet office in the park, losing my footing in the world, completely unsure of my value system and the choices I had made in my life. I obsessed about the grounding for my choices, realizing that there wasn't one and this brought me to rage over and over. So I became more of a mechanism with each passing day, losing transcendence, losing ontological space, retreating to the "safety" of the choice and the comfort of the bourgeois. Again, however, and this had happened at another time in my life, the natural price I was paying for this loss in freedom due to my self- duplicity, was killing me.

I did follow him. I did profess myself an authentic doer. But I could never seem to do what was necessary.

Anyway, this nervous, twitching, sweaty mess of a dream state kept me in bed until I heard loud voices outside the beach house. Already, families were getting into position for the day, umbrellas, coolers, towels—all of it—disrupting my solitude enough to roust me from the anxiety of the night. Now it was just the anxiety of the day.

I had messages from the sheriff, who wanted to see me again about the dead woman we had found several months ago when I had left for the Malpais to find Rachel. There were messages from some of

my local acquaintances and messages from one of my publishers.
This all meant that there'd be more administrative paperwork,
which I abhorred and which I would do anything to avoid.

I splashed some water on my face and trudged on up the hill. I
walked up the road toward town where'd I get coffee and breakfast
and re-connect with that part of me I'd put down to a nap last fall.

There you are, she said, as I walked into the diner. I smiled.

They all looked at me and smiled. Then I sat down to breakfast. I
hoped it was just a matter of days before she showed up in town —
the woman with the dark shroud who I'd had been tracking for
years. She had agreed to meet, finally, so I knew if I were patient
she'd show. I waited for her over the next several days but she did
not come.

Chapter 13

After I bought the land south of the Malpais, I'd put up a couple of tents for the supplies. Once I went down there after almost a year's absence and I discovered that the squirrels had taken over. They'd gnawed a couple of holes in one of the tents which they used as a nursery for their newly-born and I didn't have the heart to chase them out. In short, I let them have the tent and considered it a compliment that they wanted it. I just moved the supplies into the trees and spent the trip shooting beer cans.

I loved my solitude out here. It was the desert's version of the pure-white snowfield I'd experienced as a child. Once I stayed out there a couple of weeks and chanced a trip further south down into the No-Man's Land. This was even more remote and not dark and ugly like the prickly heat of the Malpais. Temperatures soared and people's skin turned to leather out there. They became isolated misfits, split off from everybody else. Their reality focused on their immediate needs—their morality reflected it. Stay out of their way and all was good. Get in their way at your own risk. Go into the desert at your own risk.

Everyone was down here to test his resolve to stay sane in nearly absolute aloneness. Even the kind of sociality that occurred here was sparse and limited, again amounting to the discharge of very basic needs for relation and a common goal of silence. But one day I headed down into the No-Man's with a full tank of gas and a truck with solid tires. I'd left most of my provisions with the squirrels so I could head out with a clear conscience.

I put my gear into the bed of the Indigo truck, headed out of the area on a greatly rutted road, and then went left instead of right, down into the sun. There were two lanes on old asphalt. Blue-gray sky. A hawk. A car going the other way. A carcass near the side of the road with some blood splatter. The wind on my face. Thoughts about the wasted time in Ravenswood. Imaginings about a future that had already always been.

I drove under the speed limit heading for a town six or seven hours down the road. It was very hot but so dry I didn't sweat. Down here the heat sucked the water out of everything—with it, life. The only exception to this was the cactus, which hoarded what little there was left. In humans, this was that little bit left over after one had made it through the gauntlets of family, school, community, and culture; that pure spot of untainted soul that some people protect from the mistreatment of others. At least that's what my belief was, and anyone could see how the things I did in my life reflected that.

Even so, when you put yourself far, far away from civilization—phenomenally, from the voices of others, you lose the dialectic. You lose moral refinement and moral complication. You lose that dividedness between your impulses and fictional accounts of the ideal that others had planted in your mind. I liked this space because otherwise I was on edge all the time.

I drank from a one-gallon water jug and wiped the excess on my shirt. I checked my gas gauge and listened to the tires. I watched for hawks. I considered the history of my interactions with the woman at The Blue Pearl. We were always starting conversations that never seemed to finish. Last time I'd been in there, we drank coffee, ate pie, and spent the night together.

Earlier today, we talked about philosophy, history, politics, and movies. We talked about school, the war, and the economy. But we didn't talk about me and we didn't talk about her. She was an enigma except for the picture of her sitting on the lap of the man. He was smiling and she was looking at him. It was in a frame on a night stand with a lamp in a darkened hallway on the way to her bedroom. When I asked her about it she dismissed the question summarily with a comment about her "other life" and then we went into the room.

After, we went to sleep in the darkest room just off of Route 66 in the western side of New Mexico, down by the Malpais, in a place that was becoming a center of gravity for me. When I woke up she was gone. Not just downstairs but gone for the day.

She'd left me a friendly note explaining that she had to drive into

town for supplies and for me to help myself to lunch, which I did.
Then I sat in the booth of the café and drank coffee. She had closed
the restaurant so I didn't have to deal with customers. She ended the
note explaining that she knew I'd be gone before she got back. That
was right before I got my truck and headed south.

The only other thing that I had in my truck was the pistol, which
I'd been carrying around since I left my hometown. Other than the
fact that I'd gotten it from my grandfather right before he died, it
only represented the possibility of relief if I ever needed it. I don't
think I had fired it more than on a few occasions but I knew enough.
I glanced at it sitting on the floor of the passenger side and kept
driving, noticing the hawks, smelling the heat. I kept driving.

Later on that day someone noticed the gun still sitting in the truck.
Hey Bub, he said. What's that gun for? I looked him over but didn't
answer. I just kept on eating and sipping at the beer. Then I walked
into the desert with it. I kept walking until my feet got tired and the
sun got to me. I woke late in the afternoon in town to a couple of
desert people splashing water on me. Are you alright? You Okay?
They got me to my feet.

I said nothing, let them splash the water, ate some of their dinner
and headed back north to my land. I built a fire and drank half
a bottle of whiskey until I started dancing and singing. I lost
consciousness again. I woke up—it must have been the middle of
the night—to a group of coyotes. I ducked my head out into a dirty-
yellow moon, clutching the pistol, drunk. I was out of my mind,
thinking about the time I'd almost shot myself out of a fugue and a
spite toward all the things that didn't seem right.

Smoldering hot alcohol breath. My joints hurt.

As the flames died down from the red-yellow to gray ember, I
looked up into the dark background behind the white specks of the
future. I felt warm inside, that even though all this searching had not
produced much, it'd be alright in the end.

I lost consciousness to the night.

Philosophical
&
Poetic
Interlude

When it stopped making sense

I let go of my desire and opted

Instead

For virtue and truth

Pushing away the noise

That pulls.

Fragmented slivers of perception

One after the other

Continue pushing each other

Away

So that vision of the Whole,

Impossible.

Thus, I am at once both lost and

Liberated; looking for signposts

Along the way

Which

Always seem heralded by the blue

Iridescence.

The dark penumbra of the Walking

Park remains forever etched in my

Consciousness. Unsure that I will

Ever return to the shadows there,

I strain to recall her face

Calling.

Mother Death. Sweet and bitter,

Soft and genuine.

Always with me speaking the

Words; there is more; there is more.

Do not be enchanted into egology.

Abjection rules.

And all the while the tall, large frame

Of admonition walks alongside.

"Couragio!"

The royalist inside falters as the

Governorship wanes.

Lost. Eroded. "Couragio!"

PART TWO

Chapter 14

Now I was ready for the dance. Now I was ready and fully prepared for something I'd wanted to do my whole life. Now I was aware of my intention and my feelings about it. Now I was ready.

Being nomadic afforded me the anonymity I needed to fulfill my life plan. I was able to move from city to city, coast to coast without being tethered to an oppressive social identity. I was someone here and a different someone there.

Watching the kill from a quarter mile had both excited me and disgusted me. The pack brought the fawn down effortlessly while its mother looked on from a safe distance. She was horrified by the precision and savagery that the universe had allotted to her realm. She had no time for sadness and quickly fled, darting away, far away from the danger, her calf now a memory.

I recall talking about it late that night—perhaps around 3 a.m.— by moonlight, with the dandy from the east coast who shrugged it off as "nature's way." Why then, I posed to myself, ought we view ourselves as different when it was clear to me that our own way was not so different?

The debate had been unresolved. Now, years later, in a different life with a different identity, I was still ambivalent about my own nature —including issues involving good and evil, rights, and the lack of a recipe for good living. I had considered the priesthood at one point, but the whole matter seemed somewhat disingenuous, at least for me, and also somewhat repulsive in its negations of what seemed most obvious and natural in men.

It seemed wrong that anyone could pronounce the moral order for anyone else. I was already confused enough with what others had indoctrinated me into early on. Yet I'd struggled with these questions for a long time, especially those relating to boundaries and borderlands. Unfortunately [or fortunately!], at this time in my life I was again presented with the questions.

I'd been killing — at least it was in my imagination – all the dirt and
filth of the city in which I lived. I wiped it out with a clean rag late
at night when I could avoid the judgments and the condemnations.
The lazy. The greedy. The lustful. Somehow, I had also been swept
into the Age of Moral Judgment, and there fit right into the practice
of assessing the behavior of others. I was not only assessing it but
finding ways of expressing it to the world at large.

I'd sought Him out because he represented the Good and the True,
the endpoint of higher levels of human striving. Like a (good) priest,
he embodied ideals of virtuous behavior and therefore our time
together was less about me healing and more about the transmission
of value. I had been killing without remorse and thought myself
"evil," so when I realized that he was going to murder me, I felt
comforted. Of course, we never openly talked about it, but I saw
it no differently from the sort of priestly excisions they did down
the street at the Church [encouraging transcendence from the
"AngelBeast," the paradigm of human frailty we had inherited].

In addition, I had the problem of being overly-sensitive, hyper-
vigilant, and perhaps a bit paranoid though not in the way that
you'd expect. My awareness was not of the egological sort, and
so my points of consciousness did not always originate from my
self—as body—but from various other points in space and time. The
raven assured me of this truth as a reminder, always appearing and
reappearing in my horizon of possibilities.

Thus, I allowed myself the luxury of being stalked by the very
oppression I became aware of at a tender age. I could feel him sizing
me up, considering my own ability for reprisal, and readying for the
inevitable parry. He was there, watching me as I would walk around
the downtown shops and cafes; watching me traverse the graveyard,
following my every move as I carefully stepped around the stones;
gazing at me as I stepped from my car, on the way to a bookkeeping
project.

I never said anything. Instead, I allowed myself to be pulled in to his pathology during the sessions I would pay for, carefully avoiding the sort of discourse of collusion and conspiracy. Still, I was drawn.

Otherwise, I'd spend time talking in the group with his "sick" wife who, it turns out, was not sick at all. In fact, she was perhaps the healthiest of all of us, living in the interstitial corridor between this dimension and the next. I'd also see her in the park, before or after my "therapy" sessions with her spouse. For me, these were separate projects—the therapy and the walks in the park, but I was the common linkage.

As I lived in my own moral "turpitude," [earnestly] engaged in my healing process, I'd started feeling the watching, the regarding. I felt judged. Gazed at. I felt pursued—not as object of desire, but as object-to-be-annihilated. The hairs on my forearms would stand up, often in the most unexpected places and times. Thus, he was able to not only be my therapist but also my stalker. Again, it was a mixed bag, both of containment (as a moral agent striving for the Platonic ideals) and as abjection (involving loss of that containment), as I could act in fragmented and inconsistent ways, depending upon the life perspective at that time.

I personally, did not believe that he had it in him to finish me off, so I allowed him the privilege of the hunt—mostly the privilege of imagination—which, of course, gave him the feeling of power, and me a counter imagination. It was an imagination of his imagination; it was a double movement of imagination, therefore. It was a dance of madness: I pretending to be in therapy; he pretending to stalk me. But it gave both of us a profound sense of pleasure that was punctuated only by his marriage to her and my friendship with her. I am sure that she was the woman in the shadowy penumbra of a lost summer, a long time ago, Mother Death.

And so he stalked. And I saw ravens everywhere. I could only hope that one would lead me to water.

Chapter 15

It only took a few hours with him for me to realize that my whole
life had been in vain, that I had unwittingly bought into the
prevailing ideology of our time. I hated him for being so cavalierly
able to cut the throats of innocent people. I, myself, was sick —
desperately so — because of the possibility that I'd been on a wrong
road for the majority of my life. That's a long road I'd been on,
and the thought of having to retrace my steps back to the "origin"
made me feel tired and weak. Moreover, it made me feel resentful
enough to consider ending the whole matter. I just couldn't see my
way clear of reweaving all of it back to the beginning and restarting.
Remaking my ship while it was still afloat also seemed improbable if
not impossible.

It seemed that I was being watched, not necessarily by humans, but
by ravens and perhaps hawks. Even in my travels when I'd step off
an airplane or drive to other cities, they'd swoop down around me.
They'd look at me and then they'd go. But their presence had been
made, burning an indelible memory into me.

My wife was sick — had been sick – for a long time which, I realized,
had enabled me to pretend that I was healthy. It was only after she
started getting well that I started losing my foundation. Coupled
with the evil that I was pursuing — in the hopes of eradication — my
life was unraveling and my choices were constricted. I wanted to
reel it all back to an earlier stage in my life so that I could make
different decisions. But I couldn't and therein was the hang-up. Life
only moved in one direction. Forward!

One of my new patients was formerly an Organization Man who
had gotten used to seeing the company doctor for his misanthropic
behaviors and obstreperous retorts. After he was fired, his attitude
became somewhat morose and subdued, although he had taken to
feeding off the lives of others through murder.

Through my own ineptitude I had been recently drawn into a most unfortunate moral quandary and had most miserably failed at it. The facts are unimportant, but what is prevailing is that I no longer thought myself a moral man. My whole safe, bourgeois belief system about uprightness had been thrown into question. This further cascaded into doubt and skepticism about the foundations and core of my very being. It had thrown me into an ontological insecurity and an existential panic, the proportions of which I had never experienced heretofore.

To further compound the problem—which I rationally discerned and rationally cogitated—one of the very people I had sworn to serve (primum non nocere) was engaging in ruthless barbarisms toward others. He had no moral compunction. No scruples. No guilt. He had no remorse and was, therefore, free in a way that I could never be. This only served to cause me great distress. Thus, I imagined (often at inopportune times and places—-church, making love with my wife, therapy sessions) twisting his throat into a piece of bloody, yielding, corrupted flesh. These experiences, of course, distracted me; moreover, they caused me a secondary and derivative kind of stress. I was, I realized, caught in an ineluctable, infinite regress of self-loathing and resentment that I had not yet experienced heretofore.

My imagination ran wild with all sorts of ways that I could resolve my unresolvable problem. It was helter-skelter and Armageddon in my soul: a double, anti-dialectic, both ironic and paradoxical in nature—a zugzwang which seemed inescapable. It was a Hobson's choice.

The ravens chattered and danced. I saw them everywhere, taking pokes at me with their stares and quips. They could hear my thoughts, which bothered me greatly as I'd walk through the city streets. Turn a corner, there's the iridescence. Start the car, there's the blue.

One day, I was so tired from all of it that I slumped back into the driver's seat of the old Mercedes, watching the just-after-lunch crowd walk the park, readying for afternoons. They were refugees from the 60-hour work week and the company doctors, unconsciously making their way from birth to the grave with little perspective about their situations.

A raven swooped down and sat right on top of the hood of my car. He sat motionless, looking at the park. Then he re-arranged himself until he was almost facing me, looking somewhat in a westerly direction. He sat and I sat and we looked at each other at the slight angle, regarding our mutual regarding. He didn't move and I didn't care. Eventually, the tension wore me down until I was just tired, so I slumped down thinking about the Malpais, the No-Man's Land, and the family cabin up north, farther than Ravenswood, deep into the mountains.

I used to go there as a kid to get away from the madness, but I had recently learned that the madness had found the north, so much so that the notion of an unblemished, fresh mountain snowfield was left solely to the imagination or to picture books about the way things used to be.

The forest had been chopped up and raped. Large corporations had moved in.

Even my own boyhood was now a sliver of a memory at best, fragmented, torn, and tattered. The only thing I had left was a vat of ideologies and teachings. Now, with my moral violation, my whole footing had become unsettled. The ideologies seemed like child poetry. My adult commitments based on those ideologies seemed like fiction. I felt like a human pendulum swinging from truth-hold to entrenchment, the ethical commitments unmoored, my coherence now jagged. It was in this chaos that I firmly resolved to kill the object of my spite in the hopes that it would purify me of my confusion. A last chance bastion of authentic stroke, I thought it would land me in peaceful green meadows.

So I began my obsession, watched the ravens, feeling resentment at my wife's recovery. I had lost my self. Thus, I began planning and obsessing, imagining the various ways that I could take my vengeance. It was only in the corner of my awareness that I recalled

Confucius's admonition that before we take that vengeance we must dig two graves. I fought like hell to keep that notion on the periphery, nipped at it like the junkyard dog that it was; screamed like a wild monkey for it to be gone.

However, given human nature being what it was, that part of me that would always be fooled by Fool's Gold was again, so I continued my obsessive imaginings about destroying the beast inside me by destroying him. I even went so far as to stalk him — with murderous intent.

But when the rubber met the road, and the wheat was separated from the chaff, I couldn't. For I was a weak man. A fool and a weak man. A working man who was a weak man, and a fool to boot. Thus, I was left to being watched by ravens, still in a moral quandary, and no less resolved [or absolved, as it were] from my resentment.

After we split apart, she and I, and after I sold everything and left, I spent many months and some years driving up and down the west coast eating tacos, reminiscing about my land between the Malpais and the No-Man's, and all that I had left from my imaginary life [in an imaginary universe] on the east coast, on the Island. This was not the Island that I had inhabited in the West; no, it was the Island that I believed I still had business on in the East, on the Atlantic seaboard.

I oscillated, therefore, between rage and depression.

Chapter 16

I could feel the blood leave my body, and assured myself of this truth as I saw the burgundy-colored droplets spill out onto the towel I had placed neatly on the hardwood floor.

I looked out the window.

I could feel my heart beating faster than normal, as I crossed the divide. This is the boundary between the motivation to save yourself at all costs [the great egology!] and the will to not care anymore come what may.

For way, way too long, I had been on a course of self-preservation, adjustment, and adaptation. There were many compromises and sacrifices, and I bought right in to every one of them in a utilitarian way, fueled by my unique ontic reality, and very little understanding of the ontological difference. My thinking, my rationality, my very reasoning, had already been structuralized and developed under conditions I didn't understand, providing me a convenient recipe for my existence.

But with my wife's recovery, my moral quandary, and my out-of-control stalking of someone I had a duty to help; with my basic sense of self awry and my core values now cluttered and obfuscated, I lost my desire for it. I, like a dog who had killed before, lost my desire for the "raw flesh" of my desires. Now, how could that happen?

The blood spilled.

The ravens watched.

I missed my other lives.

I thought about the cave under the Malpais.

I thought about the girl who ran away and opened The Blue Pearl

Restaurant.

I never figured out the identity of her "double" who had been murdered out on Falcon Island in the East.

I never figured out my association with the bourgeois.

Still, the blood spilled and I aged.

My relationships changed and I moved.

I lost my land and forever lamented about it. I always wondered about the squirrels who had claimed it. Chances are someone had eradicated them while squatting on the land.

I made it back to the "67 Club" many times over the years and it was always a different crowd there. Sometimes I stopped at The Blue Pearl restaurant and spent the night, on my way to my land, down into the No-Man's.

Still the blood spilled and I aged.

Unfortunately, I made the wrong interpretation of this loss of desire and so [wrongly] set about to claim my life. I mean to say that I set about to take my life—the life that I had claimed.

In another life I was an Organization Man, but not this one! I couldn't accept that I, too, had fallen prey to repressive ideologies and beliefs that we were all forced into every single day. I mean to say that I have this intuition that in my imaginings of being a healer, in fact, I was living a life elsewhere with a different name and a different identity.

I was still drawn to blue pearls and always felt a little jittery when I'd see one. On occasion, I'd sit and stare, touch the opaque roundness, and imagine myself elsewhere, doing something different with my life. Yellow colors caused me the feeling that I'd been here before.

Still, the blood spilled on the floor, on the towel that I had placed on the hardwood floor. It was quiet because it was a weekend, and no one I am sure was at the office building today. Intermittently, I'd stop and listen, my heart beating, the pain throbbing. Had I heard someone? Was someone listening to me? Trying to watch me through the door? Monitoring me?

I couldn't be sure so I continued the bloodletting. That is, I fully engaged in the process of letting go of my life. If I died in the process I no longer cared. At some point during this quiet, contemplative morning, I stopped and cleaned up. I sat in my office on the couch where all my patients sat—had sat—closed my eyes and let my imagination run. This seemed to be the only free space I had these days, and it too was running out, so I relished whatever there was left.

My eyes shut and the building quiet, I drifted off to sleep. Muffled voices at first filled my head with noise, but gradually became more specific, clear. And precise.

Mr. Lykeman, … Mr. Lykeman, I heard. Yes, I responded. What? I asked. Mr. Lykeman, please don't move. You've had a major rupture.

Oh my God, I thought. This again. This story about me being an Organization Man, carted off to the hospital because I could no longer handle the secure world that had been laid out in front of me was going to drive me nuts.

Mr. Lykeman, please sit still. Don't move.

Then the voice left the white room and the blue iridescence was at the window. I then pulled the needles from my hand and arm, found my clothes, and hurried out of the hospital. I noticed people looking at me—I must have appeared awful—as I fled from there.

In the distance, I could hear people calling my name. Mr. Lykeman. Mr. Lykeman, they said. I continued hurrying through the late weekday afternoon crowds, through the rain and through the approaching dark. I had no idea where I was going but I had to get out of there.

Then everything turned still and quiet. I was running just above the ground it seemed, one foot after the other propelling me to an unknown destination.

But the blood continued dropping onto the towel. By now — hours into my little ritual — the dark red liquid had splashed itself into quite a little puddle, bouncing off the fabric onto the dark stain of the hardwood floor.

I was by now petrified that someone would come by, not so much for the expected reasons, but more because I didn't want to be interrupted in my quest. I would stop the cutting every minute or so, straining my ears so to hear any interloper. Once, this must have been late morning, I thought I heard footsteps coming up the stairs so I sat motionless for several minutes. I eventually breathed a sigh of relief and was just about to continue when I heard the knocking at my door.

My heart rate jumped through the roof for this infinite moment. If I said something I'd risk that the door would open [Unfortunately, I had failed to lock it and so was at the mercy of the inclinations and will of the Other.]. If I said nothing, I'd also risk that someone would perhaps try the door to see if I were in.

I decided to say nothing. Whoever it was knocked again and waited for a couple of minutes then left. He or she or whoever it was padded down the hallway and down the stairs though I could not be sure.

A multitude of thoughts entered the door of my consciousness, some staying some fleeing; others combined into new and more complex thoughts, but they kept coming incessantly. These thoughts continue moving through my awareness quickly during the rest of the afternoon, during my demise.

Chapter 17

I knew it was going to be a long road to dig myself out of all the accumulations of the past several decades. About this, I am not only referring to material possessions. I am more concerned about the layers of the onion [in one conception] and complicated ironic semiology on the other. In my youth it had been appropriate to appropriate and to possess, but now it seemed a burden and a waste of time. I couldn't simply throw it all to the trash heap. [This is why the bloodletting, as a metaphorical gesture, could never lead to finality. It just did not make any sense.]

It'd taken me a lifetime to build an identity, and then all of the subsidiary identities, as well. I came to know that they operated as a constellation of vantage points, clustered around a concatenation of feelings, responses, intuitions, and body sensations that had been formed in the womb and somewhat beyond. It was the death instinct that had eventually won out in priority.

I woke one morning to a spider ambling across the bed sheet and a tapping at my window. In the old days I'd have killed that spider and discouraged the tapping but now I welcomed it. I let the spider walk and I went to the window, just enough to look at the tree outside. A raven was there on one of the branches, tapping. We stared at each other. I smiled. He cocked his head and studied me. I studied his iridescence. The sun shined.

Then I went to the kitchen — I'd had the walls painted a bright, provincial yellow — and sat waiting for the coffee. Of course the raven had followed me there, sitting on the sill [I'd opened it up for him.] and we both enjoyed this shared time. He eventually flew off and I looked in one of the mirrors. I think I could see a faint smile forming from my mouth.

Of course, I'd followed the "Doc's" order enough to regain the trust of my coworkers. I'd taken my medications enough to satisfy Organization medical personnel, but really it was my behavior about which they were concerned. I found that if I followed the expectation no one raised an eyebrow. One step out of line and I became a target. Armed with this knowledge, I made my plan for an exit and a retracing of steps that had gotten me to this place.

Thus, I bought an old truck and drove down the west coast. I ate the tacos and drank the beer. I watched the sun travel across the sky and I dipped my toes into the surf. I had left the Organization and took with me my interest in being a psychologist and my experiences as a bookkeeper. I could keep records like nobody's business. I remembered everything and wrote it all down.

I left.

I remember them when I left. Not a one of them looked at me or even in my direction, not even my secretary. I was leaving the flock, obviously causing major distress in the hearts and minds of everyone else. Building security was called and they had earlier tried to persuade me into leaving over the weekend when no one was there; I had resisted the invitation, preferring instead to traipse out of there early in the week during the workday.

When I walked past the company doctor's office I could see him in there with another person, a newer worker who was having behavioral issues. I smiled lightly, not too noticeably, and continued walking. I could see that the doctor noticed me by his exaggerated act of looking down, paying just a little too much attention elsewhere.

So I drove down the coast a "free" man until I got almost all the way to the border. [Note that it took me six months to make it this far.]. Then I took a small flat near the ocean and spent my time in contemplation, visiting small bookstores, cafes, and the beach. I did get to know a few of the beachcombers at that time but kept a prudent distance because of my intention to move on soon.

Quite accidentally—and to my delight—I ran into a few people I used to know from one of my old lives, many years ago. This triggered in me such a torrent of feeling and creative energy that I ended up buying painting supplies and spent several weeks drawing

and painting the resolutions of my recent history. I almost quit
eating, instead opting for water and caffeine, drawing my sustenance
from the sun.

One night I awoke in a sweat. My dreams were new, quite unlike
any others I'd ever had. It was raining, both outside on the coast,
and in the dream, from which I'd not yet emerged. I was soaked
from head to foot and it was pitch black outside except for the
fragments of the yellow moon that penetrated through the thicket
out here in the North Country.

I was shivering and confused. I had no idea where I was except that
I knew it was in the North, somewhere in the vicinity of my birth. I
could tell this by the types of pine and fir about, as well as the smell
of the mountain and the dirt. I was home. I just didn't know where
at home I was.

My clothes were torn. I was tired. I smelled of alcohol and
cigarettes. I was hungry.

I could see the lights of the town southward, both to the east and to
the west, but mostly south.

I was in a field of some kind with a fence off in the distance. I turned
a full 360 degrees and could see the fence traversing the perimeter of
the field, lit by the yellow moon peering through the mist.

I got up from the soggy ground and almost fell down again, weak
in my legs. I stood up straining to stand up straight and tripped
over a hard object. I looked down and saw what appeared to be a
gravestone. I looked around through the rain and realized that I was
in a cemetery. It was the one on the north side of town. This was the
old part of town, the part that had been there for as long as the town
had been a town.

I surveyed my situation. It was late. Dark. Wet. I saw lights from
houses a good walk from here. I saw lights from the town. But I was
alone and it was late, so for a brief moment I felt a bolt of anxiety rip
through my soul like a hunting blade.

It was very similar to the one in the East where they had buried the girl who had been murdered. It was very similar to the one I used to drink booze and smoke cigarettes in when I was young. It was very similar to the one in the City where I used to live. This was many years ago when I was trying to figure out the basic propositions about morality, science, and my aesthetic sentiments. But in all of them I felt the same: I felt comfortable and at home. In all of them I felt like I had come back to the house — the safety of my boyhood home — at the end of a long summer Saturday; And no matter what I had done or what had happened, I knew that everything was going to be alright.

So I'm in this graveyard drenched to the bone, out in the middle of nowhere [I discovered that I was bleeding, hungry, tired as well.] but I felt like I did as a teenager when I had just come home at the end of another long day after causing trouble. I felt the rain on my face and I gave thanks. I felt the rain on my forehead and I smiled. Somehow I knew I was home even though I did not recognize anything around me.

It was like walking out of the cave in the Malpais, thirsty and tired, but home to the hot desert sun. It was like walking away from a gang of hoodlums who could have killed me but didn't. It was like walking out of examinations. The police station. A hospital. My boyhood home. A girlfriend's bed. I was home here in the cemetery in the nagging rain and all.

I sat and cried. Then the rain stopped and I got up to walk to town.

Chapter 18

After another summer in the East out on the Island [and this time I finally stayed at the Well-To-Do, the hotel and restaurant for the guests who liked the fat trimmed from their steak], I concurred with the old waitress's suggestion that it was time for me to move on, that I'd done everything I needed to do out here—except get old and fat. So I sold most of my things, including the beach house, paid off all my debts to the locals, and left. The only thing I hung on to was a string of rare blue pearls I had gotten from my mother's side of the family.

It's perhaps not that they weren't worth anything. It's more about the lifetime of memories they represented. The false hopes. The unmet dreams [thank God!]. All the people who I had known who had died. The truth is that by now I'd forgotten most of them, the memories being a worn-out vinyl record one plays obsessively [remembering more than actually hearing].

I promptly headed to a town I regularly went to—the one with the park I'd sit at and contemplate life—to sit and contemplate! Of course, the woman was long dead, and so was her husband, one of my ex-therapists. The path around the park was still dirt, packed down hard like a sedimented life. It was still gray, as well, always appearing so even on a sunny day [I had never figured this out; it was still one of the great mysteries in my life.].

I sat on the same bench I had sat on for many years and watched all the other people walk around the park on the same dirt trail. Walking. Walking. Walking forward to their eventually expirations. Just like me. However, the difference for was that my destiny was in the Great Place in the north. I just had to make the right steps to get there. And it would not be a straight line.

Drinks at the 67 Club. Several nights—even weeks of them—at The Blue Pearl Restaurant [I brought my string and gave them to her. I thought this was appropriate, all considered.] I knew she would probably look at them twice and then put them away but it seemed fitting. It was more about the act of giving them away than anything else that I cherished.

I knew I'd never see her again, which was something I wasn't sad about. We'd had our time and it was over. She'd eventually grow old, sell the diner, and move back to a city where she'd find services for the elderly. In the case that she didn't, I am sure she'd find a new home. We all do, all the time. So that last night with her I really enjoyed myself, as I always did doing something that I knew would soon be over. It was an opportunity to be grateful for what would no longer be. So we had steak and a lot of it. We sat and talked late into the evening, watching the flames in the old fireplace die down, as we died down our relationship [which had never been more than a few meetings every year even though they were important to both of us.] But it felt special and real. Very Real. This was because we both felt we could share the full truth without reservation, something lacking in most relationships.

We sat watching the fire, talking mostly about our childhoods, healing even then in the 12th hour of our friendship. We both knew that when I left in the morning we'd never see each other again. We both knew that we'd die in our respective ways and most likely not even think about each other at that moment, which was true of most relationships that people accumulate. In that final hour, one rarely thinks of them.

So the flames died down and we talked openly. She reminded me of my best friend—a girl—back in grade school because of the total and utter openness between us. I guess it was because the vulnerability was transitory and ephemeral, tolerable in its passing state. We fell asleep in each other's arms and neither one of us dreamed. We woke up early and ate breakfast together, silently. We drank coffee and ate breakfast and then I packed my truck. She thanked me for the pearls and we hugged. I walked around the perimeter of the restaurant, looked to the north—which was where I was eventually headed—and then to my truck. We hugged for the last time, shedding tears both of us, and then I drove away. I never saw her again.

I then drove to the county seat, sold my land, and said goodbye
to the Malpais. It would be there long after I passed and for some
inexplicable reason that gave me comfort. Then I headed west to the
coast. I had some things I had to do there, some final business, and
then I'd head north for the duration.

At this point there wasn't much to resolve except for the outstanding
issue of the recordation of my thoughts and my leftover resentment
at having chosen to be the led instead of the leader, the sick instead
of the healer.

I wanted to be the doctor. I had wanted to be the doctor.

But the time for this option was now over as all opportunities
eventually become.

Instead, I had to live with the memory of my choice to be part of the
herd for most of my life, swimming in ideology, traversing the world
in shackles. I had striven for such a long time to find solidity in a
world without any; to find emotional and ontological in a world that
only snickered at the attempt.

I still didn't know who I was. What I did know was that I had just
about detached from the project and was looking for comfort in the
simple things, like when my truck started on the first go, or when I
ran on the beach with my dog. I included a good meal in this as well
as a sunny day. And so forth. All else seemed not only redundant but
a severe distraction as well.

In my drive across the desert, I lost the will for stoffe — "stuff."
More fundamentally, I lost the will for teleological thinking, which
I had spent most of my life pursuing. This was, of course, a cultural
product of existential fragmentation and the loss of self that came at
the crucial time we all enter into the world of the Other.

By the time I reached the ocean I was very tired and therefore slept
for a very long time.

Chapter 19

I woke up in the cemetery again, but this time I was a child and it wasn't raining. I'd had dreams about ravens all night and was worried that the principal of the school was really going to punish me for getting the ink all over the pure yellow walls of the lavatory.

I fell down and lost consciousness. I woke up in another place. All I could see was a little boy, five years old maybe. I recall the words coming at me like arrows [later like bullets]. Something was wrong. There was a place I was supposed to be but didn't know where and therefore couldn't prevent the words. There was something I was supposed to do but I didn't know what.

I just remember looking at the boy and the words coming at me and then the leaving. It was a strange environment: a yellow kitchen that was too bright, whose walls seemed to enclose us in a container from which I could not escape; the dog on the rug looking, watching; the phone ringing now and again, interrupting the soap opera; the lunch at just the right time.

So it was the dog, the mom, and this boy I continued to see. There was the Father who'd come around, bringing a tension and stress I didn't understand. The situation itself was an oddity. I'd later classify it as gothic in the sense that we were remote from the city, alienated from the center of things. And I always remember being perplexed and discombobulated. I was uncertain and hesitant in my approach to the whole matter because—as I later realized—I would never have chosen it.

The walls breathed a heaviness that drained our spirits into the earth. Little sound was allowed to enter because she had everything all closed up. Everything happened on a schedule, in a certain way, and at a certain time. And this occurred for an unknown duration, so when I saw the boy I was startled, intrigued, and afraid, and relieved, all at the same time.

Disgust percolated up from the belly of the home and contributed to the emotional palette of the family, along with all the other feelings that got pushed down. Mostly it was a Manichean split between "good" feelings, when someone got his way, and "bad" feelings, when someone didn't. The distemper came from me and the dog. It was like an experiment that someone had volunteered me for—without a firm end date and without clear rules.

The boy I continued to run into always seemed mortified though I didn't have words for it at the time. The reality of it had been so squeezed down, so compressed, that it could have been the head of a dime or a pin, a page from a magazine or the screen of the television.

It was dark, shadowy, and opaque; it was nascent.

He'd fill his time playing his part in the whole of it, learning the gestures, the rules, and the presencing/submerging movements he was called to do.

She'd do what she would do—the cooking and the cleaning and the rest of it and I'd be there. There were the words and the noise and the tension and I'd be there. And I'd keep seeing that boy, encouraged for this and dissuaded from that. But I'd watch his reticence carefully as he'd respond in ways that followed the system: The Organization. Myself, I would slink off to the Unknown Place, which was free from the noise and the words and the gestures.

One time there was a babysitter—someone on a temporary basis who was a member of the family—who came by wearing a blue dress and a string of blue pearls. She was gentle. Quiet. Unassuming. She was there without being there.

Hi, she greeted, opening the subterranean caverns in the field of silence wide for passage. With the Mom gone and the Father at work there was a golden silence; even the dog could rest.

The two hours with the woman excited such possibility and such communion of souls. Laughter filled the air. Eye contact was so tongue-and-groove. And the little boy was gone, somehow vanished

for the time, retreating to the shadows and corners of the little house
[in repose, I suspect], unnecessary.

Given that this was on a weekend day—a Saturday I believe—and
that it was sunny, we had been allowed a walk, frolicking near the
railroad tracks that moved into the distance, later listening to the
river nearby. Of course she had been warned, so although we could
smell the sweet honey of freedom we could not eat of it. However,
this possibility burned a place in my heart and soul, later to serve as
fulcrum for all courageous endeavors.

Back at the house before it became filled with noise and tension,
we all sat on the porch watching a few ravens watch us from the
tree. We watched and they watched and all was silent. The golden
sun wrapped itself around us. The blue skies adorned everything.
And I watched her face and the string of blue pearls she wore. And
I watched the ravens carefully. And I retreated when everyone got
home. I went away to the No-Mans' Land in my soul—the crucible
of truth—down into the vessel beyond space and time from which
truth arose.

And I woke up in a cemetery, in a town somewhere, watching a little
girl and her mother place flowers on a grave. In the distance I could
hear the swooshing sound of a river, a steady roar of life that filled me
with such vital hope, such promise of tomorrow. There was no little
boy out here and no Mr. Lykeman, cajoled and pressured into forty
years of service without even a handshake at the departure door.

I could see other people around as I walked toward town but they
didn't pay me much attention. It was no matter: I enjoyed the rays
of sunshine and the blue sky, attentive for a sign of a hawk, perhaps
even a raven. I turned around once and saw the little girl following,
feeling a familiarity in her face though I couldn't place it.

I crossed the railroad tracks at the north end and headed downtown
to a restaurant called The Golden Rule. When I crossed Main I felt
the watching and of course it was a raven but it wasn't iridescent
blue. Instead, it was actually a golden yellow, translucent shimmer—
and hard to see. There were people milling about, late lunchtime in

the early afternoon, warm outside.

Of course the raven said nothing but I felt something coming from him to me. It was nothing I could put into words but I knew that it had always been there and always would be no matter the form, the time, or the place.

Shadows struck themselves across the old red brick of the still-young town as I was shooed into The Golden Rule by the hard-to-see raven. Then he flew off and I took a seat in the back. No one noticed me and I wasn't served but I sat there anyway, feeling a sense of belonging. I felt a sense of home.

I heard of the rivers and the spring run-off and the recent drownings. I heard of a new government and an optimistic economy. I heard talk of new businesses from the East, the advent of the modern corporation, and profits beyond comprehension. There was a group of fly fishermen talking loudly about their trip. There was a little girl sitting with her mother, watching me. She was looking at me while she ate her sandwich. Such beautiful sadness was pouring out of her but I resisted the urge to approach. There was a familiarity but it was oblique and opaque and I couldn't place it. Rachel, … her mother said. It's time to go.

As they rounded the corner, I came out of the restaurant. The girl had dropped something so I hurried to get to it.

It was a black and white photograph of a family. On the back was the notation, "Lykeman family." One of the individuals in it looked a great deal like my Father. I looked up from the photo and the girl and her mother had vanished.

Then I woke up in the cemetery and saw my name on the gravestone in front of me. This time it was raining again and I knew that the rivers had overflown their banks—all three of them. Thus it was a wet soggy mess and somehow I had again ended up in the town graveyard, amongst the headstones and the green grass, in the north end of town.

I held tightly to a string of blue pearls and I had no idea how I had gotten them.

Chapter 20

Mr. Lykeman, please calm down. The priest will be here soon and you can talk with him.

Please, Mr. Lykeman, just take it easy. You'll be able to speak with him in just a minute.

Then the priest entered, a big hulk of a man a full head taller than most. He smiled and we talked about everything except my impending change. He regaled me with new stories, motivated me with new admonitions, and chastised me again for mistakes already made and reconciled. Then he left, saying the usual:

Couragio! Couragio!

I again tried to sit up but they gently pushed me back as my wife entered the room. Melina, I said, as our eyes met. I've missed you so. She smiled and we held hands for a few minutes before they came to get me.

I will always love you, I said. She smiled.

Then I watched the clock on the wall and the raven at the window. It was the golden yellow one, pushing up against the window sill, which had been snapped shut. I could see him out there sitting, tapping on the wood, which led me to believe that everything would be alright.

The procedure was painless, they had assured me. It would be like a long sleep and when I awoke everything would be different, free from the angst and the responsibility and the requirements.

In the "procedure," they said, I'd feel just a pin-prick sensation as I entered the doorway. Then I would be bathed in golden yellow sunlight, walking a path filled with sounds from my childhood, perhaps from a time before I had started to see the little boy wherever I went, before I began to retire to the shadows.

Where's the priest? I asked. What priest? The attendant replied.

Where's my wife? I asked. Wife? Someone queried.

Then they wheeled me into a different room at the end of the hall and I felt the pinprick on my skin.

At the same time, the little boy collapsed on the floor, dead. He had a peaceful look on his face as he walked to one of the three rivers, the most dangerous one that had taken many lives earlier this year in the spring.

Chapter 21

I walked out of the darkness of the cave in the Malpais, into the sunlight, and I smiled. My phone was ringing and I answered it immediately.

Mr. Lykeman, the voice said. You are wanted at home.

Then I made the long trek back.

Heart-of-Fire

Heart-of-Fire is an imprint of EPIS Press dedicated solely to fiction, poetry, and other literary production that is related to psychoanalysis, phenomenology, and critical theory/deconstruction.

EPIS Press
31 Fort Missoula Rd., Ste. 4
Missoula, MT 59804
epispublishing1@gmail.com